by

MICHAEL FESSIER

TURTLE POINT PRESS

© 1993
Turtle Point Press
Turtle Point Road
Tuxedo Park, New York 10987, U.S.A.

First published in United States
by Dial Press, 1948
First published in Great Britain
by Allan Wingate (Publishers) Limited, 1949

All rights reserved, including the right to reproduce this book
or portions thereof in any form.

LIBRARY OF CONGRESS CATALOG CARD NUMBER: 92-061472
ISBN: 0-9627987-1-1

Cover illustration from
Scènes de la vie privée des animaux: Études de moeurs contemporaines
by Grandville, J. Hetzel et Paulin, Paris, 1842
Design by Linda Corrente
Typesetting by AeroType, Inc.
Printed in the United States of America

Clovis

*C*lovis cracked an almond, nibbled it, then ate a raisin. He turned a yellow-irised, black-pupilled eye on his companion, August Von Lerner. His voice was bitter.

"I," he said, "am weary of all this. I desire to go away from it all."

"Ach," said August, "so many times this has been coming up of late."

He sighed in sorrow and gazed out past the cool veranda to the beautiful Brazilian coastline, watched the waves break upon the shore. "Such a lovely spot," he thought.

"Why are you not happy, my little one?" he asked.

"As you know," said Clovis, "I resent being referred to as little one. Aside from that, what *is* happiness? Is it spending the hundred or so years of one's life in unceasing changelessness, with the only hope of variety being death?"

August Von Lerner shuddered.

"Do not mention death," he pleaded. "It is far in the future for you. For me it is a mere handful of tomorrows."

1

"You have a certain measure of my sympathy," remarked Clovis coldly. "But sympathy is no antidote for boredom. I am bored."

"But," insisted August, "there are the Greek and Latin to read. There is chess."

"Inasmuch as the Greeks and Latins have found nothing new to say for centuries," snapped Clovis, "they also bore me. And as for chess, you no longer afford me competition."

"That, alas, is true," admitted August unhappily. "But it gives me so much pleasure in losing to you, you are so brilliant." He wrung his hands. "Oh dear, oh dear, oh dear," he said. "Is there *no* way of keeping our domicile, our little home together? Oh my little one, my pretty one, my adored one."

"That is another reason for my impatience," said Clovis angrily. "I will no longer tolerate your addressing me in terms of feminine endearment. I am male."

"That is merely *your* opinion," said August. "As you know, there is no positive method of determining your sex, unless you lay an egg."

"Well," Clovis pointed out triumphantly, "I have yet to lay an egg."

"That is purely negative evidence," said August. "It is not conclusive. You may be androgynous. You may be sterile."

August was quite right.

As everyone knows, it is impossible scientifically to determine the sex of a parrot save for the advent of an egg.

And Clovis was a parrot.

For centuries the ancestors of August Von Lerner had been breeding parrots for intelligence, as well as speaking ability. Their reason was not scientific at first. The early Von Lerners were acrobats and, even then, their profession was held in lowly esteem by other performers. Troubadours, minstrels and court jesters, when angry at one another, were often given to pronouncing the direful curse: "May all your progeny be equilibrists."

Smarting under this contumely, the ancestral Von Lerners had decided to get a new act. Inasmuch as Russian performing bears were all the rage, the worthy Germans decided to go their Muscovite brethren one better. They conceived the notion of presenting performing birds. Now, as everyone knows, the brain of the parrot is larger and more perfect than that of any other kind of bird, being better developed and having more convolutions, in addition to boasting a superior anterior lobe. So the parrot was decided upon for the experiment.

In those days the only parrot available was the Bittacus, or Indian parrot. It proved adaptable as a talker but its prejudices were against it. Birds imported from a Mohammedan sphere of influence were prone not to get along with those of Hindu leanings. For a while the experiment languished.

So the Von Lerners decided to move their enterprise to the New World, away from religious prejudices. They founded the town of Oporto Freitas on the coast of Brazil. There they began breeding parrots by the score, by the hundreds, and finally the thousands, selecting the most promising and selling the rest. Having done their best with the native Amazonian parrot, they imported Cuban parrots, African Greys, Mexican Red-heads and Mexucab Double-yellow-heads, cross-breeding them with Maracaibos, Hondurans, Cartagenians and Australian Shells, culling them carefully and retaining the best of the species for further experimentation.

As the years went by the breeding of parrots became not just a means to an end but a goal in itself. The Von Lerners were obsessed with the ambition to produce a paragon of parrots, a perfect species that would be able to think as well as talk. It was a laborious, often heart-breaking task. Advances were made only to be wiped away by an injudicious bit of cross-breeding, and the painstaking work of years was lost. But, by now, the Von Lerners were scientists, not showmen, and time meant nothing to them. The work of one generation was handed on to the next and faithfully pursued toward the one paramount goal—the perfect parrot.

Finally, minor successes were achieved. After years and years of unrewarded effort there came into being a bird who could count up to a hundred and could distinguish and name correctly the primary colours. Further breeding produced a parrot who could do all those things and, in addition, tell the time, do simple arithmetic and read easy words such as 'cat,' 'dog' and 'rat.' From there on it was merely a matter of a hundred years or so and two more generations of Von Lerners until the selected birds had passed from the grammar school to the high school equivalent of human intelligence. Then, after a half century's delay, the college type was produced.

The two most erudite of this group were the parents of Clovis. They sickened and died soon after the egg was hatched. The same malady struck the rest of the parrots and they, too, began to die off. It seemed that in breeding parrots for intelligence, the Von Lerners had neglected to retain in them their native hardihood and resistance to disease. Finally, only Clovis, of all the parrots, remained alive.

On Clovis, the Von Lerners lavished all their care and attention. They imported the cream of Europe's crop of teachers and a crew of specialists was on hand at all times to guard his health. Clovis did not disappoint his tutors. He was precocious from the start, assimilating knowledge in great gulps and demonstrating unmistakably that this was no mere feat of memory. His ability to reason was equal to that of humans.

By the time Clovis was twenty years of age, the Von Lerners began to sicken and die. Their disease was diagnosed as psitticosis and nothing could be done to save them. At last only August, of all the Von Lerners, remained alive.

August was a well-educated vacuity. His reasoning powers were rather dim. The convolutions of his brain were few. His anterior lobe was shrunken. It seemed that, in breeding parrots for intelligence, the Von Lerners had reversed the process in themselves. They had become an inferior species.

ugust gazed unhappily at Clovis who, after his repast, was daintily dipping his claws in a finger bowl.

"This discontent of yours has been growing of late," he remarked. "I seem to be the cause of your dissatisfaction. What is there about me that displeases you?"

"You are articulate for one thing," replied Clovis. "You are articulate to the point of distraction but you never say anything worth listening to. Perhaps at first I was mildly interested in your chatter because of its naïveté, but even that element finally became oppressive. Having once revealed your shallowness of perception you have insisted on reiterating it daily, the same weary thoughts, the same false emotions, the same puerile beliefs."

"But without conversation," pleaded August, "what would there be for us?"

"For me, heavenly peace," declared Clovis. "Conversation should be a constantly renewed attempt to reach higher and hitherto unexplored intellectual ground. With you it is a daily drowning in familiar quicksand. How often have I longed for you to hatch one new idea, one mewling, puking infant of an idea. It might be a two-headed monstrosity of an idea but at least it would be an idea and we could nourish it and cherish it and relieve the tedium of this existence.''

''You seem to derive great satisfaction from hurting me,'' complained August.

''Forgive me, then,'' said Clovis, not unkindly. ''But when one allows sentiment or emotion to mitigate the truth the two get together and breed a lie.''

''Happiness, maybe,'' said August, as usual unsure of himself, ''consists not in lies but, perhaps, the avoidance of disturbing truths.''

''A fool's philosophy,'' sniffed Clovis. ''I do not wish to avoid truths, especially the disturbing ones. Right now the disturbing truth is that I am bored and I require a change.''

''Perhaps I can do something to relieve your discontent,'' suggested August. ''Could I procure for you a wife, perhaps? Or a husband, as the case may be.''

''Again you repeat yourself,'' snapped Clovis. ''I know what I am. I know how I feel.''

''But one cannot always be too sure, even in the human race,'' said August. ''There are variations, you know.''

''That does not concern me,'' said Clovis.

''Especially it concerns you,'' insisted August. ''Nature must have been in a jocose mood when she conceived parrots. There is—ah—no differentiation, as it were. Especially is this noticeable in the male sex. There is no—'' He blushed and then went on. ''In our generations of experience as parrot breeders, the only method we ever devised to attain a fertile egg was to place a group of birds in one cage, willy nilly. Some fought, others ignored one another and still others showed great congeniality. These latter we knew were mates and we paired them off in seclusion. That is the way we selected your parents. But still, inasmuch as no one actually witnessed the laying of the egg, we never did know which was your mother and which your father.''

''I consider all this extremely indelicate and embarrassing and I'll hear no more of it,'' declared Clovis. ''How would it set with you if I were to discuss the manner of *your* conception?''

''I have heard it discussed many times between my father and mother,'' said August morosely. ''Each seemed to have attached a certain amount of blame to the other.''

''I can well understand that,'' said Clovis waspishly.

''Perhaps at last I have solved it,'' said August, happily ignoring the remark. ''Perhaps I have solved the problem both of keeping you interested, and of finally determining your sex. I'll secure several other parrots. The one you show affection for will be your mate. Whichever one of you does *not* lay an egg will be the male and entitled to the name of Clovis. You know it was *you* who selected that name, out of your admiration for the great king of the Franks.''

''That I did,'' agreed Clovis, ''out of my admiration for the king of the Franks and out of my knowledge of myself. And if there is to be a mate for me, which is a subject I have been considering of late, I shall select her myself.''

''How in the world could you do that?'' asked August.

''How do others of my race find mates?'' asked Clovis. ''Do they have them delivered in crates? Do they have to undergo the peculiar methods your family developed to induce them to conjugate in captivity? No, they find their helpmates in their natural environment, out in the free jungle.''

''Then it is your desire to visit the jungle, select a mate and bring it back here to live with us?'' asked August. ''I would approve of that.''

''I didn't ask your approval,'' said Clovis. ''And it is not my intention to bring my mate, providing I find a worthy one, back here to live.''

''You propose to live in the jungle?'' asked August, horrified. ''Why?''

''That is my destiny,'' said Clovis loftily. ''I shall join my people, live with them, teach them, and lead them to higher things.''

''But your education,'' wailed August. ''The work of generations of Von Lerners—wasted on a jungle.''

''Is education ever wasted on a jungle?'' asked Clovis, sternly. ''And for what purpose did your ancestors intend me?''

''I don't know,'' admitted August. ''The original intention has grown vague in my mind. I suppose they just got into the habit of breeding parrots and couldn't get out of the rut.''

''I prefer to believe differently,'' declared Clovis. ''It stands to reason that I was intended for a more worthy destiny than to remain here and go into an intellectual moult. My duty is with my people.''

Clovis was obdurate against all the arguments and pleadings of August.

Finally August capitulated.

"Far be it from me to deny one his destiny," he said. "Go and with my blessings, my little loved one. But, when there is nothing to do, will you think of me perhaps?"

"If there is nothing else to do," agreed Clovis.

August watched Clovis pigeon-footing out of the room and down the path and he wept great salt tears.

*C*lovis was walking down a dusty road, placing one foot almost cross-wise in front of the other, making slow progress but enjoying it. He tasted unfamiliar odors, heard strange exciting sounds and wondered why he had never ventured away from the Von Lerner estate before. He supposed it was just another indication of the stifling influence of August Von Lerner. August had never been away from the family compound in his life. "Poor August," he thought, "a cauliflower if there ever was one—with legs." He continued at a leisurely pace, drinking in all the sights with a slightly cocked, appreciative eye.

Clovis had gone about a mile when he became aware of a sniffling sound behind him. He turned and saw a brownish mongrel dog which had been following him. The dog stopped as Clovis stopped.

"Well, what do you want?" asked Clovis.

The dog pricked up his ears and slanted his head at Clovis.

"Go away," said Clovis. "I do not desire company."

The dog wagged his tail tentatively. He was used to hearing parrots talk, but there was something different about this one. He came a little closer and sniffed. Clovis bit him on the nose. The dog howled and retreated. He sat for a while, eyeing Clovis speculatively. He finally ventured a low growl and Clovis, startled, backed away. This was all that the dog required. Courage flowed back into his craven heart. He advanced, belly low, hair bristling, and emitting ferocious, blood-curdling threats.

Clovis, out in the world for the first time, realised something that had not occurred to him before. Used to commanding the hulking August, their difference in size had not seemed to matter to him. Now he understood that mere bulk had its advantages. He backed away and ruffled his feathers.

"Go away," he commanded, rather weakly.

Still the dog advanced, gaining courage at every step. He was slobbering a little at the mouth.

"I command you to desist," croaked Clovis.

The dog opened a red mouth fringed by nauseous yellow teeth and Clovis decided that his last moment had come. He felt sad about ending his brave pilgrimage here on this dusty road at the jaws of this loathsome creature and he almost wished that he had not left home. Then he decided to be brave about it. If death must come, then let it come, and he'd meet it courageously, as Clovis, the king after whom he was named, would have met it.

Just as he felt the hot wind of extinction on his brow, Clovis' quick wit came to his aid.

"Lie down," he commanded.

The dog hesitated a moment.

"Lie down, you," said Clovis and repeated some coarse obscenities he had overheard the Von Lerners' gardener use in addressing his dog.

Clovis' enemy was not so much impressed by the command to lie down as he was by the extremely free flow of profanity. This, he realised, was no mere bird. When the parrot of his household swore there were but a few expletives and they were delivered flatly and without meaning. But, behind *this* stream of vituperation, there was purpose and direction. The dog sat down and looked unhappy.

Clovis followed up his advantage. He unleashed a new stream of curses and then said *"lie down"* with such complete authority that the dog obeyed and lay trembling.

Now that he had accomplished it, Clovis considered what to do about his conquest. He felt a little tired and he remembered that, when at home, he had only to command and August would carry him on his shoulder. Clovis, now completely sure of himself, climbed upon the dog's back.

"Get up," he commanded.

Resigned, the dog got up and trotted off down the road. It was the direction Clovis wished to go, so he relaxed and enjoyed the ride. It was, he considered, a much better means of locomotion than walking. He wondered why it hadn't occurred to him to have August buy him a dog.

"The power of the intellect will always prevail," Clovis told himself and nipped the dog's ear. The dog broke into a gallop and Clovis fluffed his feathers in the refreshing breeze. They came to a cross-lane that attracted Clovis. "Turn in here," he commanded. The dog kept straight ahead at a dead gallop. Clovis issued another command with the same result. "The power of the intellect," he amended his previous statement, "will prevail only if its commands are understood. This animal understands only elementary things and therefore will not suit my purpose."

14

He hopped off the dog's back and returned to the lane of his choice. He followed it for some distance and then, feeling hungry, turned in at a small thatched farmhouse. He went round the back and found an old man and woman sitting in the sun. They paid no attention to him. He cleared his throat.

"Hello," he said. "I hope you find this day as delightful as I do."

"All days are alike," said the old man.

"That may be so, in one sense," said Clovis. "But, aside from that, I am hungry. Would you be so kind as to provide me with food?"

"What a disgusting parrot," said the old woman. "He's got a running off of the mouth. Any other parrot would say "Polly wants bread" and let it go at that."

"Indeed," said the old man, "everyone talks too much these days, including parrots. It isn't like when I was a boy."

"I apologize for my verbosity, then," said Clovis with wounded dignity. "May I have food?"

"No," said the old lady. "Go get your own food."

"But," said Clovis, "I am Clovis."

"Go get your own food, Clovis," said the old man.

"I am not used to such treatment," declared Clovis.

"Go where the treatment is better, Clovis," said the old lady.

"Food," said Clovis, "is always provided me. I have never had to bother with such matters. You see, I am a person of distinction, of education."

"Well, with the taxes we pay, somebody should get an education," said the old man.

"We, on the other hand," pointed out the old lady, "have no education. But we have a hut and we have food and we know how to provide it for ourselves. So don't stand there giving yourself airs."

"It was not my intention to give myself airs," said Clovis. "I realise that we all do not have the opportunity I have had for advancement but—"

"Scat or I'll pull out your tailfeathers," said the old man and he made a lunge for Clovis' posterior. Clovis scuttled back, then walked off, muttering to himself.

As Clovis plodded along he realised that the old couple had seen nothing remarkable in his vocabulary nor in his powers of reasoning. They were annoyed, rather than impressed, that a parrot had stood before them and conversed with them in highly intelligent terms.

"Well," said he philosophically, "I suppose only the gifted can comprehend a miracle. To the dull brain everything is commonplace."

He came across a small girl, who sat by the wayside playing with a rag doll, and stopped to pass the time of day with her.

"How do you do, my pretty one," said Clovis.

"Thank you," she smiled. "You're pretty, too."

"Why do you play with that odd bit of rag?" asked Clovis.

"It isn't a bit of rag," said the girl. "This is Isabella and she's beautiful."

"In your imagination, perhaps," agreed Clovis. "But you must realise that, in reality, Isabella is merely an old mop rag."

16

"She's *not* a mop rag," said the girl resentfully. "And I don't think you're pretty any more."

"Juvenile reasoning," smiled Clovis. "I say you're pretty and so you think I'*m* pretty. I disagree with you about a bit of rag and I am no longer pretty."

"Besides I don't like you," said the girl.

"In an intellectual discussion," said Clovis with a superior air, "the element of personal likes and dislikes is not permitted. The question being discussed is that bit of rag you fondly imagine to be a person by the name of Isabella."

The girl regarded him gravely for a moment.

"I'll bet," she made her pronouncement, "that you think you're smart."

"Of course I'm smart," said Clovis.

"Well I don't think you're smart," said the girl.

"Why not?" asked Clovis, amused.

"Because, if you're smart, why are you talking?" asked the girl. "Why don't you fly like other parrots?"

Clovis was stunned. Never in his sheltered life had he felt the need of flight. He had always walked or August had carried him. In this respect he was the same as his uneducated domesticated cousins, who seldom fly unless under compulsion.

"And if you're too stupid to fly," the girl pressed her advantage, "you're too stupid to see how beautiful Isabella is."

"All right, then," said Clovis with dignity, "I shall fly."

On the first attempt he fell flat on his beak and the little girl laughed happily.

"Do it again," she urged.

Then Clovis' intelligence came to his rescue once again. He remembered what he had observed about the flight of other and lesser birds and realized that everything depended on the take-off. He took a run at it this time, flapped his wings and was airborne. He circled the girl once, just to show her, and then soared into the blue.

As he winged his way toward the distant green jungle Clovis tried to conquer his ignoble resentment of the little girl.

''He who repays good counsel with anger is a fool,'' he told himself sternly.

And he flew on, feeling a little foolish.

lovis sped over miles of verdant jungle, enjoying to its utmost the freedom of flight. All space was his. He had discovered a new realm. He was master of the universe.

"Although I seriously doubt it," he told himself, "there may be, among men, scholars more erudite than I. There may be more profound thinkers, ones whose horizons are broader. But I, alone among the philosophers, can fly."

At that moment a DC 6, bound for Rio de Janeiro with passengers and mail, roared across his bow. Caught in the backwash, Clovis had a bad time of it. He was tumbled head over claws through the air, the earth spun around him and his brain reeled. Finally, he regained control and flew on even keel, watching a few feathers drift away from him.

He gazed with rancor at the disappearing airplane.

"Ha," he said, speaking of the pilot, "if it were not for a motor and petrol and mechanical wings, he would be a clod and he would fall like a rock."

Thus reassured, he continued his journey. He followed the course of a winding river for several miles and then decided to rest. He spiralled down to the branch of a tree and then gazed out over the vast, unending jungle.

"This," he said, "is my domain. At last, Clovis, you have come into your own."

His dreams of grandeur were interrupted by raucous voices coming from a nearby tree. Clovis flew over to investigate. The tree was filled with brilliant-plumaged Amazon parrots feasting on fruit that was unfamiliar to Clovis. He settled on a branch which placed him in prominent view of the others.

"Greetings, my people," he addressed the others. "I am Clovis. I have flown many weary miles to come to you."

This created no stir among the busily feeding birds. They squawked contentedly and continued to eat.

"Hear me," said Clovis, louder. "This is an event in your life. This is your dawn of destiny. Clovis is among you."

The other parrots found the fruit far more interesting than the announcement. Finally, Clovis whistled shrilly and this either had the desired effect or else the parrots had had their fill of fruit. A few began to pay attention to him, to move closer. Others followed and Clovis had an audience.

"I know my presence here may be strange and puzzling to you," Clovis admitted. "But it is no spur-of-the-moment notion on my part. For many years I have been considering this move. I have come to show you a better life."

The birds were staring at Clovis' plumage, trying to decide what kind of a parrot he might be. Although he was obviously a stranger and not one of their species, they felt no inclination to attack. They were just curious.

"Although I am not one of you," Clovis said, "I am of your kind, I feel a kinship between us. I have gladly relinquished the advantages and comforts of civilization to offer you my services. Although it is taken for granted that you shall want me to lead you, I am most humbly yours to command."

He bowed and the others still stared curiously at him.

"Are there any questions?" asked Clovis.

There were a few puzzled squawks but definitely no questions.

"Come, speak up," commanded Clovis. "Pray, do not be self-conscious. Consider me one of you."

One of the parrots, obviously the leader, moved closer and uttered a few squawking phrases at Clovis. This was utterly unintelligible to him.

"Come, come," he said, "speak up."

The squawking phrases were repeated.

Then suddenly Clovis realized that *he* had been speaking human talk.

The other bird was speaking parrot talk.

And they could not understand one another.

It was no use for Clovis to try Portuguese, Latin, Greek or any other of his vast repertoire of tongues. The sudden, the awful, the incredible truth came over him. In breeding parrots for human intelligence, the Von Lerners, the accursed Von Lerners, had bred them away from knowledge and understanding of their own species. He, Clovis, could speak a score of languages but he could not speak his own.

The leader of the parrots tried a few more remarks, doubtlessly, Clovis felt bitterly, dropping down to a juvenile idiom as he tried to make himself understood. Then he shrugged his wings and turned to the others as if to say, ''What an ignoramus!''

The others laughed gaily. It was obvious that they considered Clovis, the great Clovis, a dolt, a bumpkin; worse than a backward child. They continued their good-natured banter for a while and then, wearying of the sport, flew away in pairs and groups. Finally Clovis was left alone, brooding over his Waterloo. A Waterloo, he reflected disconsolately, that had no Austerlitz to lend it dignity or meaning in retrospect.

Seeing him there, alone and unhappy, a kindhearted female with a vivid red spot on her forehead flew back to Clovis. She clucked sympathetically to him, nudged him with her wings and indicated that he should follow the others. Clovis was too broken in spirit to demur. He had no plans for the future.

Together with Red-Head, Clovis arrived at the dense part of the forest where dwelt the parrots. It was dusk and they were settling down for the night.

''Just like chickens,'' thought Clovis. ''Their day ends with the sun. They live but to eat and sleep.''

Clovis, used to electric lights, was not accustomed to retiring before midnight. It was during the dark, quiet hours that he had done his most profitable studying. Now with the soft noises of the jungle about him he was restless and ill at ease. He wished he had a book to read, any book.

As the hours droned along, Clovis began to nod. His exertions of the day were finally taking toll and he was sleepy. Just before he dropped off into a deep slumber he was conscious of a touch on his cheek, a soft touch as light as a feather. He thought he heard a tender sigh and then he slept with a faint, sweet, musky odor in his nostrils.

When he awoke at dawn, Red-Head was not in sight and Clovis decided that perhaps it had just been a dream. But what a delightful dream!

The flock left for a distant eating place and Clovis followed discreetly in the rear. He didn't want to be drawn into an attempt at conversation with anyone. He watched the others and learned how to eat food in its natural state, finding that it tasted better than when served on a platter. What distressed him, however, was the lack of variety. Beside fruit and nuts he had been used to rare cheeses, hard-boiled eggs and, delight of delights, milk liberally seasoned with cayenne pepper.

Toward mid-afternoon, Red-Head appeared. At first she stayed at a distance from Clovis and then she began edging closer to him. Clovis watched the maneuver with palpitating heart and finally decided to meet her half-way. He edged closer and closer to her and presently was at her side. She plucked a fruit, turned her back to him and began to eat, completely ignoring him. Clovis worked himself around to the other side and again cold wings were turned to him. He cleared his throat several times, trying to attract attention. She gave him one cool, impersonal look and flew away.

That evening, Clovis trailed the flock back to the dense forest with a heavy heart. He sat, alone and ignored, until sleep finally began to overcome him. Then, in that split second between consciousness and oblivion, he thought he heard an ineffably sweet sigh, and there was the odor of musk in his nostrils.

When Clovis awoke in the morning the odor was still with him. And so was Red-Head, perched next to him on a limb. A bright eye was looking into his. Slowly and ever so slightly, it winked.

As if it had been discussed and agreed on, Clovis and Red-Head paired off that day. As they winged their way over the jungle, Clovis' heart almost skipped a beat. And it was not from romance. He had just realized that, in Red-Head, he had the instrument by which he might yet attain his rightful place among the parrots.

As the flock settled into a fruit tree, Clovis piloted Red-Head to a secluded spot nearby. She followed docilely, even eagerly. He settled on a limb and she roosted beside him. She did a peculiar little dance, holding her head low and clucking softly. Clovis had an idea what she was up to but he decided it could wait. The spirit of his crusade once again burned within him, squelching other and lesser flames.

"I am going to teach you to talk my language so that you can converse with me and translate my wishes to the others," he said, knowing that she could not understand. "First we will start with simple things. Try to follow this." He pointed a wing at himself. "I am Clovis."

Red-Head cocked one at him speculatively. This, she decided, was indeed a strange bird. What a way to begin a courtship! Well, she shrugged, if that was the way things were done wherever *he* came from—

She listened attentively and, being eager to get on with the game, she learned quickly.

24

"I am Clovis," she said triumphantly, pointed a wing at herself, and waited quivering with expectation.

"No," said Clovis in exasperation. "*I* am Clovis." He pointed a wing at her. "*You* are Red-Head."

She looked disappointed. What, another preliminary? When was this stranger going to get down to cases?

Clovis repeated the lesson over and over again. At last Red-Head pointed a wing at him and said, "I am Clovis. *You* are Red-Head."

She went into her odd little dance, clucked invitingly and watched him hopefully.

Clovis was exasperated beyond patience.

"For the love of heaven," he exploded, "you talk just like a parrot."

And then he realized that she *was* a parrot and could learn human words but not understand the meaning of them.

"I'm sorry," he said. "I suppose we'll just have to reverse the process. I shall learn *your* language, as uncouth as it sounds. Perhaps that is best after all, for then I shall be able to address the entire flock at one time."

Red-Head didn't have the slightest idea what he was saying but she pretty well understood her dance wasn't going to get her anywhere. She roosted a small distance from him and regarded him glumly.

By exercise of much patience, Clovis finally made Red-Head understand what he required of her. She considered it a lot of nonsense but decided that if this *must* be another required preliminary to her goal, she'd make the best of it. The first words she taught Clovis ranged from salty to downright lewd.

"Keep your mind out of the nest," Clovis commanded. "Language is too precious a gift to waste on such subjects."

Although thoroughly disagreeing, Red-Head complied with his wishes. In practically no time at all Clovis was master of parrot talk.

"Now that I have taught you to speak," said Red-Head expectantly, "what is it you wish to say?"

"You have been patient," Clovis told her. "And you shall be rewarded. You will find the goal worthy of your efforts."

"It'd better be," said Red-Head. "When do we start?"

"Soon, soon," said Clovis. "But we must move carefully. My campaign has many ramifications."

"Good," commented Red-Head.

"We must prepare the other patrons to accept their destiny," said Clovis.

"They don't need any preparation, they've accepted it," said Red-Head. "You'd be surprised at what goes on around here. And, incidentally, what have the other parrots got to do with it? Just what *have* you got on your mind?"

"A new social order," declared Clovis.

"What's that mean?" asked Red-Head suspiciously.

"I shall give my race the benefit of my wisdom," said Clovis. "I shall lead us all to a better way of living."

"You mean you know a place where there's more fruit, more nuts, more berries?" asked Red-Head, discouraged at the turn the conversation was taking.

"We do not live by bread alone," said Clovis. "There are the things of the soul. But if you speak of earthly things, then I can promise you many practical benefits. An easier existence, more comforts, more luxuries."

26

"We've got everything we want now," said Red-Head. Then she gave him a meaningful look. "Or, at least, *the others have*," she went on.

"Pah, what do you know of civilized living?" scoffed Clovis. "You with your primitive jungle habits. Why, where I come from, I have every advantage that a human being does. I partake of food such as you never have imagined. My every wish is obeyed. Even my cage is of German silver. I have books to read, paintings to look at, music to listen to. I have come to tell you of those things and to lead you toward that more worthy condition of life."

Red-Head gazed thoughtfully at him for a moment then took to her wings and flew away.

"At last she understands," Clovis told himself. "She can't wait to tell the others."

At first Clovis was inclined to follow Red-Head. Then he decided to delay his visit to the flock and thus make it more dramatic. "Let her first prepare them for my coming," he told himself. A great surge of joy swept through his being. "At last, Clovis," he said, "you are on the threshold of your destiny."

His pleasant flow of thought was interrupted by faint squawks in the distance. They came closer and he realized that the parrot flock was bound in his direction.

"Ah," he told himself, "they have come to greet *me*. That is more fitting and proper."

Then he began to make out words from the wave of sound that was speeding toward him.

"Traitor! Deceiver! Betrayer! Judas Parrot."

It was incredible. His ears must be deceiving him.

But the horrid words became unmistakably clearer as

the flock approached. Soon the parrots were swarming and circling about him and he heard, shriller than the rest, Red-Head's voice, the voice of the woman scorned.

"He wants to deliver us over to men. He wants to put us in cages. He told me so with his own tongue," she screamed. "He's a traitor and betrayer."

Frantically Clovis lifted his voice to explain, to tell them that the cage represented not captivity but civilization, but the more he spoke the worse he made things for himself.

The anger of the parrots reached fever pitch. They threatened to claw out Clovis' eyes, to eviscerate him, to spill his life's blood. And always there was the shrill voice of Red-Head urging them on.

Clovis realized that, although their anger was genuine, their desire to spill blood was not so fervent. Still he knew that his continued presence might drive them to the fulfilment of their threats.

Sick of heart, he took to his wings and flew swiftly away, followed by the taunting laugh of Red-Head.

"In addition to which, he's a sissy," she screeched.

lovis flew on and on, heedless of direction or destination. His world was ashes, his dreams dust.

After hours of flying, he wearily alighted on a tree limb and gave himself over to bitter soliloquy. So poignant was his grief that he expressed it aloud.

"Alas," he cried to the unresponsive silence, "alas, how wasted—how wasted, indeed, are words of wisdom when cast on the pagan ear. Like seeds planted in barren soil, left to moulder and rot while poisonous weeds thrive and flourish. Alas! Alas! Alas! Of all the fates devised by the evil that rules our destiny, to be misunderstood is the worst by far."

As Clovis talked, a small, brown, naked Indian had crept silently close to him. In his hand he carried a spear. It had not been his intention to stalk a parrot. He was hunting a lizard for his noon-day meal. But the flow of Clovis' words interested him. He had heard that white men sometimes paid many beads for birds who could say only a few words. This parrot seemed to possess an inexhaustible amount of them.

"Alas," Clovis wrung the cry from the depths of his suffering soul, "what is to be my fate?"

The small Indian provided the answer. He took his spear and struck Clovis over the head with it. Clovis fell senseless to the ground.

Later that afternoon, the Indian arrived at the spot where he had left his wife and small son, both naked.

"Oh, so you finally found food," cried the wife. Then she looked closer at what her husband carried in his hand. "A parrot," she said, disgusted. "Is that all you offer your family to eat? A miserable parrot?"

"He is no ordinary parrot and he is not to eat," said the husband. "This parrot speaks many words. I have been told that white men sometimes pay much for such birds."

"Ah, there you are—the man I married!" snapped the wife. "The visionary! While other husbands work hard and conscientiously to provide for their dependents, what do you do? You dream of getting swiftly wealthy. And while you dream, we starve without even a lizard to put in our bellies. Look at your son, oh man of great wealth. What have you to offer him?"

"Nothing," sulked the husband. "Nothing right now. But if I happen to run across a white man and he happens to desire this bird and has the wealth to pay for it, the future of your son is assured. Then he will thank his father for having looked beyond his nose."

"Well, I suppose we'll have to make the most of it," grumbled the wife. "Wring the bird's neck and we'll put him in the pot. Although he is too tough to eat, at least I can make a nourishing soup for our son. Oh, if only we had a few grasshoppers to go with it."

"No, no," cried the husband. "You cannot boil our future into soup. Give me time. I will go again into the jungle and return with food—some white ants, at least."

As the argument raged on, Clovis lay on the ground, his feet tied with a leather thong. He fully understood what was being said, having studied all native dialects.

"What irony!" he said unhappily to himself. "What a cosmic jest! For generations the Von Lerners devoted themselves to producing me, the epitome of culture, the paragon of wisdom, the utmost in refinement. All to what purpose? Here am I, bound. A captive in the dust, my precious intelligence to be extinguished, my life force to be drained off to nourish one small, rancid boy for a few hours. Soup stock!"

By dint of hard reasoning and a few well-placed kicks and cuffs administered to his wife, the small Indian temporarily won the argument.

Shouldering his spear, he went forth into the jungle. The small boy pulled a tailfeather out of Clovis' posterior and sucked on it for a while. Then he discarded it as lacking in nutritive value. The woman built a fire under a small earthen pot and eyed Clovis.

"She won't even make good soup," she said, discouraged.

"Ah," thought Clovis, "the final irony. In the same breath again to be addressed as a female and also to be deprecated as a potential of soup."

He thought of the perfidious Red-Head.

"If my purpose had not been so noble, had I been thinking of myself instead of all parrotdom, at least I could have proven—at least I could have experienced—" He sighed. "Even that has been denied me," he said.

And then the small Indian returned in triumph. Behind him he dragged a huge sloth.

"Food," he cried. "Sustenance. Now, my good woman, what of the man you married? Is he not a hunter among hunters? What now of your carpings? Behold your husband, the conqueror."

"Oh, shut up," snapped the wife. "You were just lucky. To capture a sloth all one has to do is to find one stupid enough to have fallen out of a tree. He can't fight, he can't run. All one has to do is knock him over the head with a stick. Mighty hunter, eh? You and this sloth are cousins."

"Well, anyway," grumbled the husband, "it is not everyone smart enough to find a sloth that has fallen out of a tree so hard that it was unnecessary even to knock him over the head with a stick."

The man proceeded to dismember the sloth with the tip of his spear. As he cut off hunks of meat the woman roasted them over the fire. The three Indians ate voraciously, drooling and spilling juice over their naked bodies. Clovis watched, slightly nauseated.

"In any event," he said philosophically, "there appears to be some justice in the world. Providence in her inscrutable way has caused a sloth to die so that I, Clovis, may live. What a small price to pay for the survival of my intellect."

After having feasted, the small Indian slept. Then, after having slept, he gathered some twigs and began to weave. Clovis watched and realized that his captor was constructing a cage.

"Even that," he decided, "is far better than having the essence of me inside that small boy's belly."

The Indian finished the cage, untied Clovis' feet and thrust him within. Now that Clovis was in the cage and supposedly out of his reach, the small boy became interested in him. He began poking at the bird with a small, sharp stick. Clovis dodged as best he could and held his physical damage down to a minimum. But the wound to his pride was enormous. Coldly furious, he waited until the boy became bold enough to thrust his finger into the cage. There was the sound of crunched cartilage and the finger was withdrawn, streaming blood.

The woman took a stick and beat Clovis almost into insensibility. She would have killed him had it not been for the interference of her husband.

''White men do not pay for dead birds that cannot talk,'' he said and took the stick away from her.

''I tell you that bird is evil,'' she said. ''Mark my words.''

''Careful,'' Clovis told himself groggily. ''The power of the intellect is to no avail when it is caged. Until you have your freedom you must conduct yourself with circumspection. Your marvellous brain is your only friend and it will not serve you well if beaten into a jelly.''

The woman turned to her husband.

''Weave a basket for what remains of the sloth,'' she commanded. ''We must be on our way.''

''I am in no mood for travel,'' replied the man. ''Besides, if we stay here and eat the sloth there will be no need to weave a basket, for there will be nothing to carry.''

So they stayed there until the sloth was eaten and then moved on, carrying nothing except Clovis in his cage. From the start the journey seemed to be under an ill omen.

Game became more and more scarce. Finally there was not even fruit to eat. The woman constantly nagged her husband and he became too hungry even to kick her in retaliation.

"It's that bird, I tell you," the woman insisted. "There is something evil about her."

After the fourth day without food the woman again insisted that Clovis be boiled for soup. This time the man was too dispirited to resist, and the pot was again placed over the fire.

"Now is your supreme test," Clovis told himself. "Think, Clovis, think, else you have seen your last day."

Clovis did think. He thought frantically and then memory came to his aid. It seemed to him that the spot where he was destined to become soup was vaguely familiar. Then he realized that it *was* familiar, only he was seeing it from a different perspective. The first time he had seen it was when he had flown over it in his retreat from the other parrots.

"Desist," he called to the woman. "If you will but listen to me, you shall have food in plenty before the night is over."

The woman turned to her husband.

"What is that parrot saying?" she asked.

"Your ears are as good as mine," he said. "The parrot promises us food."

"How does she know our language?" asked the woman.

"I told you it was an exceptional bird," stated the man. "Be kind enough to shut up and listen."

"I have flown over this territory before," Clovis told them. "I remember seeing a spot not far from here that is teeming with game of all sorts. Also there are fruit trees in abundance.''

"I wouldn't believe that parrot if she was my own mother," declared the woman.

"Silence," roared the small Indian. He turned to Clovis. "Where is this place?"

"Continue south for a mile or so," instructed Clovis. "You will find a river. Follow the river downstream and it will lead you to the spot of which I speak."

"She's lying," declared the woman. "She's trying to lead us into a trap."

"And, if you please," said Clovis, "I am not to be referred to as "she." I am a male."

"All the more reason to doubt you," declared the woman.

There was another long argument and again the man won out by application of vigorous blows to the person of the woman. They followed Clovis' instructions and finally came to the spot he had described. Game was abundant and so was fruit.

"I told you so," gloated the husband. "Indeed, he is a most remarkable bird."

For three days the Indian family indulged in an orgy of eating. They even remembered to feed fruit to Clovis. Finally satiated with food, they lay near his cage and slept for twenty-four hours.

When they awakened, Clovis cleared his throat and addressed them.

"Now that I have saved your lives," he said, "would it not be fitting and proper for you to give me my freedom?"

"What, and lose the fortune I propose to make when I sell you to a white man, if I ever see a white man?" asked the small Indian in astonishment.

"That is base ingratitude," declared Clovis hotly.

"Where is your sense of justice? In the name of all the humanities I call on you to release me. If you refuse, only evil can follow such a betrayal."

"Now he promises us evil," said the woman. "Now, for the first time, I begin to believe him."

"Did not I speak the truth when I told you of this place?" asked Clovis.

"That is another thing," said the woman. "How did you know about this place? Since when was it given to a parrot to tell human beings how to find food? Since when, by the way, was it given for a parrot to speak our language and say things that make sense?"

"If what I say makes sense, then what quarrel could you have with me?" asked Clovis.

"That's the way I feel," said the husband, and belched contentedly.

"That is because you are stupid," asserted the woman. "This parrot, this bird, converses with us in our language, it speaks as logically as a human being, it leads us to food. It saves our lives. Does not that mean anything to you?"

"What does it mean?" asked the husband, alarmed at her tone.

"It means that the bird is possessed of an evil spirit," declared the woman.

"How could I be possessed of an evil spirit and still save your lives?" demanded Clovis.

36

''If you had not been possessed of an evil spirit we would have died of starvation,'' declared the woman triumphantly. ''That's simple logic.''

''Now that you put it so concisely, I see what you mean,'' the husband said. ''I *do* believe this bird is evil. What shall we do about it?''

''My mother taught me that the only way to rid anything of the evil spirit is to burn it,'' said the woman. ''That is what we must do to this creature here.''

''As much as I dislike losing the fortune I might have made from the bird, I feel I must agree with you,' said the husband, who was full of food and craved excitement.

Ignoring Clovis' bitter denunciation of them, the Indian husband and wife placed a number of twigs about a small stake. They tied Clovis to the stake and were busily striking sparks to start the fire when a white man, followed by native bearers, came on the scene.

The white man was a small-time trader, returning from a profitable trip into the interior. He inquired as to the Indians' intentions toward Clovis and was distressed when the matter was explained to him.

''I hate to see anything tortured,'' he said, ''even a parrot. Look, I'll give you these if you'll let the poor creature go.''

He extended a string of beads. The small Indian seized them and danced joyfully.

''See, did I not tell you?'' he shouted. ''Wealth. At last.''

The white man unbound Clovis and placed him on a nearby limb.

''You're free,'' he said.

"Thank you, sir," Clovis said. "Your generosity shall not go unrewarded. If the warming memory of a great service done to humanity may be considered recompense, then that you shall have in great measure."

The white man goggled at Clovis.

"My gawd," he breathed, "he talks a blue streak."

"And now I bid you good-day," said Clovis and started to flap his wings for the take-off.

"Oh no you don't, my bucko," said the white man.

He grabbed Clovis by the legs and held him tightly.

"You're worth a fortune, you are," he said happily.

So once again Clovis had talked himself into a cage.

All that day, Clovis was joggled and jostled by the native bearers as they carried him in his cage. The white man marched ahead, whistling happily, dreaming, as the small brown Indian had, of untold wealth. At night a fire was built and the white man placed Clovis near the flames.

"All right now, my bucko," he said. "That speech of yours was pretty pat. If fitted the occasion like a glove. Did you know what you were saying or was it a coincidence?"

"It was no coincidence," admitted Clovis. "My remarks were from the heart. But, it seems, my gratitude was premature, for you, too, have imprisoned me in a cage."

"Glory be," said the white man, delighted. "What kind of a parrot are you?"

Clovis gave him a brief resume of his antecedents. The white man listened with rapt attention.

"And now," said he in conclusion, "perhaps you should tell me about yourself so that we may resume this discussion on a plane of mutual understanding."

The white man stared at Clovis, fascinated.

"I can't get over it," he said. "A parrot that talks like a man and *thinks* like a man. The wonder of the age!" Then he shrugged. "As for me," he said, "my ancestry can't compare with yours. My name is Thaddeus Campo, known to most as Thad. There was no thought or purpose behind my breeding. I just happened and it so happened I wasn't wanted. I've been on my own ever since I can remember and I remember a lot of things I'd rather forget. Technically I'm an American but actually I'm a citizen of the world. I came here looking for my fortune, and in you, Baby, I think I've found it."

"In the first place," said Clovis, "I resent being addressed as 'Baby.'" In the second place you are in error if you think there is money to be made from me. I am no mountebank. I shall not allow you to exhibit and exploit me, if that's what you have in mind."

"That's exactly what I have in mind," said Thad. "And how do you propose to prevent me from doing it?"

"Simply by refusing to co-operate," said Clovis.

"It isn't that simple," said Thad. "Did you ever hear of the hot-foot?"

"No," said Clovis.

"Well, Baby, your education is not yet at an end," said Thad pleasantly. "The hot-foot is accomplished by applying matches to the tender soles of the feet. If your soles are not tender, the same procedure will work on other parts of the anatomy."

"But you wouldn't do that," said Clovis.

"Oh yes I would," declared Thad. "You just name something I haven't done."

"But you're civilized," said Clovis. "You're tender-hearted. Why, when the Indians were going to burn me, you paid them not to. How could you possibly inflict upon me the very fate from which you rescued me?"

"It's simple," said Thad. "When the Indians were going to burn you, there was no profit in it for me."

He rolled over and went to sleep. Clovis sat awake, thinking deeply.

"This is another time when my intellect must guide me," he told himself. "There is no use appealing to the man's better nature because he has no better nature. Boiled down to its essence my predicament is this: I am in a cage. I must get out of the cage. But how?"

After a great deal more reflection, Clovis began to gnaw at the thongs which fastened the bars of his cage together.

The next morning the journey was resumed. Thad walked alongside the native who carried Clovis.

"Morning, Baby," he said cheerfully. Then, as Clovis refused to answer, "Oh, come off it, Clovis. There's no reason in the world why we shouldn't be buddies. The only thing that stands between us is a few scruples on your part. How about it? Shall we be pals? Partners?"

Clovis maintained a sullen silence.

"Okay, then," said Thad, "but you're going to be surprised at how fast scruples melt away under the heat of one tiny match."

Clovis, who feared fire more than anything else in the world, shuddered. Whenever Thad was not looking, Clovis gnawed at the leather thongs.

As the journey continued, Thad tried to break down Clovis's reticence. He talked animatedly about civilization, about New York. He described life in the great metropolis, painting it in gaudy colours. He also told about the people, how they lived, the peculiar things they did and said. Clovis did not answer but he listened with interest. Perhaps he should go to New York and study those people. Perhaps there he might find an application for his great knowledge. Maybe there his destiny awaited him. He was determined, however, to make the trip without Thad Campo.

Eventually the party reached a small sea-coast town. Thad dismissed the porters and, with Clovis in the cage, started along the docks seeking passage home. They passed a ship on to which were being loaded scores of animals, hundreds of snakes, and thousands of parrots. Clovis severed the last thong, pushed aside the bars and leaped from the cage. Before he reached the ground he was in flight. Shouting wildly, Thad ran after him and, not watching where he was going, fell off the dock into the water.

Clovis flew to the deck of the ship and wandered about until a second mate seized him and placed him in a huge cage with hundreds of other parrots.

"For the first time," thought Clovis, "I welcome captivity. Now let Mr Campo find me."

In almost no time at all Thad Campo, his clothes dripping harbor water, appeared on the deck. He wandered back and forth, closely scrutinizing the captive parrots. Clovis had no difficulty in concealing himself among his many fellows.

"All right, Clovis," finally said Thad. "I can't see you right now but you can hear me. It's a long voyage home and I'm going to stay on this ship until I find you. And if I don't find you on the ship, Baby, I'll track you to the ends of the earth.''

The second mate came around and stared at Thad.

''Who're *you* talking to?'' he demanded.

''A parrot,'' said Thad lamely.

''There are a lot of parrots on deck,'' said the officer pleasantly. ''Just which one are you going to track to the ends of the earth?''

''Name's Clovis,'' said Thad.

The mate lifted his voice.

''Clovis,'' he called. ''Will you please step forward? There's a gentleman here wants to speak to you.''

The captain came forward, regarding his mate with a hard, cold eye.

''On the stuff again?'' he inquired.

''Oh no, sir,'' said the mate. ''Not a drop.''

''But it seemed to me you were addressing a parrot— as if you expected the bird to understand you,'' said the captain.

''I didn't really expect him to understand me,'' gulped the mate. ''But I found this guy here talking at the parrots and threatening one of 'em to track him down to the ends of the earth and I was just joshing him.''

''Indeed?'' asked the captain. He turned questioningly to Thad.

''The man's crazy,'' said Thad. ''Why would I want to track a parrot down to the ends of the earth?''

''I wouldn't know,'' said the captain. ''Then just why did you come aboard?''

''To purchase passage to the States,'' said Thad.

''Well, we don't take passengers,'' said the captain.

''Especially passengers who look like you do. Now will you please leave the ship? You seem to have an adverse effect upon my mate.''

Thad was escorted off the ship and Clovis breathed a sigh of relief. His relief was short-lived, however, for, just after sailing, Thad reappeared, skulking among the parrot cages.

''Clovis,'' he whispered. ''I know you can hear me, so listen carefully. I'm a stowaway. Nobody knows I'm aboard. So I'll have all the nights, all the nice long nights, to track you down. Oh, I shan't do anything real serious to you. You're valuable to me, you know. Perhaps I'll content my-self with pulling a few tailfeathers out. And then there's the hot-foot, of course. How do you like that, Clovis?''

''To use one of your own crude terms,'' Clovis' voice came out of the darkness, ''I think you're a jerk. To use another phrase, you have tipped your mitt. So you think nobody knows you're aboard, eh?''

Clovis raised his voice in a perfect imitation of the Captain's.

''Ahoy,'' he shouted. ''All hands on deck. Come on the double.'' He lowered his voice. ''How do you like *that*, Thaddeus?'' he inquired.

''Look,'' begged Thad. ''Maybe we can make a deal.''

Several men came running on to the deck.

''Stowaway,'' shrieked Clovis.

Thad cursed softly and concealed himself behind a roll of canvas.

''Behind that roll of canvas,'' Clovis bawled. ''Look lively.''

Led by the mate, several men dragged aside the roll of canvas and revealed Thad crouching on the deck.

44

"Well, well, well," said the mate happily. "So we meet again. I suppose you realize that you're a stowaway, don't you?"

"I'll pay," said Thad.

"Oh no," said the mate, "you'll work. How you'll work! And below decks, in the black gang. In this climate it's going to be really awful."

As he was dragged aft, Thad's voice rose in a roar of rage. "I'll get you for this, Clovis," he said. "So help me."

Late that night, the captain stood before a mirror, a glass of rum in his hand. He looked at his reflection and frowned.

"I'd swear that it was my voice giving those orders!" he said, and gulped his drink.

oon after the steamer docked in New York Clovis and several other parrots had been placed in a medium-sized cage and dispatched to the pet-shop proprietor who had ordered them. As the truck rolled off the dock, Clovis took one last look at the ship.

"Farewell, Mr Campo," he gloated. "I have seen the last of you."

Down in the hold of the ship, the mate was forcing Thad to wipe grease off the very greasy engines as a condition of his release.

"I'll tell Clovis you were asking for him," said the mate as he started topside. "Any particular place you'd like to meet him?"

"I'll meet him," promised Thad. "I'll meet him some-time, some place, and when I do—"

At the pet shop, Mr Tanakas, the owner, was putting his purchases into individual cages. He paused as he spied Clovis.

"Such a beautiful bird," he murmured. "And what an odd species. Well, I'll have no trouble selling you. Come on, pretty girl."

Clovis had half a mind to bite Mr Tanakas, and then he changed it when he remembered his fate at the hands of the Indian woman.

Mr Tanakas placed Clovis in a smaller cage and snapped the catch.

"From one prison to another," reflected Clovis. "Ah well, there is time, a plethora of time. If I am to get along with humans, and that seems to be my destiny, I must observe them, study their ways. Certainly there is no better vantage point for that than from a perch in somebody's parlor."

Clovis had reconciled himself to being sold. But he had decided ideas as to whom he wanted to be sold to. Miss Eulalia Pomphres discovered that the second day after his arrival at the pet shop.

Miss Pomphres swept into the shop, demanding a parrot; not just any parrot but a superior parrot, an intelligent parrot, a parrot of gentle breeding.

"In addition to which," she said, "her feathers must be such as to harmonize with my parlor wallpaper."

Mr Tanakas attempted to interest her in several birds but she would have none of them. Finally she spied Clovis.

"Oh, that one," she cried. "She'll be perfect."

Mr Tanakas studied Clovis' gaudy plumage and wondered what kind of parlor Miss Pomphres was running. Then he went into his sales talk.

"An excellent choice," he said. "A truly remarkable parrot—a rare breed of the species Marabellis."

This was a species invented, at the moment, by Mr Tanakas.

"Does it talk?" asked Eulalia.

47

"Talk?" exclaimed Mr Tanakas, who had not heard Clovis utter a word, "just like a phonograph. Just like a radio even. Without the commercials."

"Well, why isn't she talking?" asked Miss Pomphres suspiciously.

"She doesn't talk before strangers," Mr Tanakas explained. "Right now you are a stranger, but you will not be for long, of course."

"Of course," agreed Miss Pomphres. "Animals always like me. I have a way with them."

She went up to Clovis' cage and began to coo at him. Mr Tanakas wandered away to another part of the shop, not wanting to be too near in case Eulalia thought up any embarrassing questions as to why the bird did not respond.

"Oh she's dis the tweetiest ittle dirl," mouthed Miss Pomphres. "Aint oo?"

"Gad," thought Clovis. "Better to have been made into soup than to be owned by this atrocity."

"Aint oo a pitty, pitty ittle dirl?" repeated Miss Pomphres.

Although a serious scholar, Clovis had not confined himself strictly to the classics. Among his courses had been one in native American idiom. In addition to that the talk of the sailors during the long voyage had done much to enrich his vocabulary.

"No I ain't," he snapped. "I'm a lousy, dreat big boy."

Miss Pomphres' head snapped back as if it had been fastened to an elastic band.

"What?" she gasped.

48

"If you buy me, I'll chew you to ribbons," Clovis promised her. "You gawdamned slab-sided, spindle-shanked old bitch."

Miss Pomphres stood with her lower jaw flapping like the wing of a wounded bird. Then she screamed like a horse in its death throes and galloped to the rear end of the shop.

"Did you hear what that parrot said to me?" she demanded of Mr Tanakas.

"No," said Mr Tanakas hopefully. "Did she say *something*?"

"No female'd talk like that," said Eulalia. "It isn't a she. It's a he."

"How do you know?" asked Mr Tanakas.

"He told me so," said Miss Pomphres. "And *then* what he said!"

"Tell me," asked Mr Tanakas anxiously.

"It wouldn't bear repeating," said Miss Pomphres primly.

"Go ahead, tell me," begged Mr Tanakas. "I won't tell anybody else."

"Well," said Miss Pomphres, "you *should* know the kind of language your parrots're using. He called me a gawdamned, slab-sided, spindle-shanked old—old—old five-letter word!"

"Did he?" asked Mr Tanakas, not daring to believe his ears. "Did he really?"

"He most certainly did," said Miss Pomphres.

"What a parrot," gloated Mr Tanakas. "How'd he know how many letters are in that word?"

"I thought you didn't hear what he said?" remarked Miss Pomphres suspiciously.

"I didn't," said Mr Tanakas.

"Then how do you know *what* five-letter word he called me?" demanded Eulalia.

"I just guessed," admitted Mr Tanakas.

"You're guessing too close to the truth and it's no compliment," snapped Miss Pomphres. "I'll never come into this shop again as long as I live."

As she passed Clovis' cage he emitted a low whistle which further speeded her progress to and out of the door.

"That," said Clovis to himself, "was no way for a scholar to talk. Still there was a great deal of satisfaction in it. It may be that the American idiom will serve me well."

Mr Tanakas came over to Clovis.

"Did you say all those words?" he asked. "Did you call that slab-sided old bitch a bitch or was it only her imagination?"

"Of course I didn't," said Clovis crossly. "It was only her imagination."

"That's what I thought," said Mr Tanakas, disappointed.

He went over and started feeding some goldfish. He paused and scratched his head. Something bothered him but he couldn't quite figure out what. He went on feeding the fish.

Clovis was almost purchased three more times during the next two days. Each time he managed to say or do something that discouraged trade. Then Miss Ewbanks came into the shop. Miss Ewbanks was a Sunday school teacher and she had conceived the idea of teaching a parrot to sing psalms as a means of encouraging attendance among her reluctant juveniles. This she explained to Mr Tanakas.

"Catholic or Protestant?" asked Mr Tanakas with a straight face.

"What do you mean?" asked Miss Ewbanks.

"Well, this Sunday school," said Mr Tanakas. "What denomination is it?"

"Oh," said Miss Ewbanks, "Episcopalian."

"Good, good," said Mr Tanakas. "All of my parrots are strictly Protestants, every one of them."

"Oh, lovely," said Miss Ewbanks.

"What's this business coming to?" Mr Tanakas muttered as he wandered away from the woman. "First they gotta match wallpaper and then they gotta be Protestant psalm singers. Good God, all it used to be was they hadda know how to cuss a little."

Miss Ewbanks interviewed several parrots and found all of them lacking. Finally she approached Clovis, who had overheard the conversation with Mr Tanakas. As she came closer Clovis began to hum softly, sweetly. Miss Ewbanks paused, transfixed.

"Why I do believe this one already knows a hymn," she said to herself. "How wonderful. It must be the influence of our dear missionaries."

Clovis hummed a for a moment longer, then changed to a tune he'd picked up on shipboard. Finally he began to sing the words, in a low pitch, especially for Miss Ewbanks' ears:

"Oh the ministrels sing
Of an English king

A thousand years ago.
He ruled his land
With an iron hand
But his mind was weak and low."

Miss Ewbanks tried to place the hymn but it found no response in her memory.

"Anyway," she said, "it seems to have a good moral. Probably it's intended to encourage thinking on a higher plane."

Clovis continued:

"His only earthly garment
Was a dirty undershirt
With which he could hide
His royal hide
But he couldn't hide the dirt."

"Rather crude," said Miss Ewbanks, "but still it *does* encourage cleanliness."

Clovis went on:

"Oh a neighbouring queen, a gay colleen,
A gay colleen was she.
She longed to play in a kittenish way
With the king across the sea—"

At this juncture, Miss Ewbanks knew the worst. As Clovis went on to finish the song, she wanted to flee but she couldn't. She was rooted to the spot until all the verses, with all their enormity of evil, had been sung.

Then she went to the rear of the shop, slapped Mr Tanakas' astonished face and fled from the place, never again to be her sweet, trusting self.

Mr Tanakas came forward and gave Clovis a suspicious look.

"I don't know what it is," he said, "but there's something about you that isn't doing my business any good. If it happens once more you're going to find out what ant poison tastes like."

Then Miss Grobney entered. She was an exquisite Dresden doll of a little old lady with soft curls that were almost blue-white. Her voice was well modulated and refined. Clovis liked her immediately.

"Good-day, Madam," said Mr Tanakas. "Is there something I can do for you?"

"Yes, I believe there is," said Miss Grobney. "Do you, by any chance, have a Ming vase?"

Mr Tanakas was taken aback.

"This," he said, "is a pet shop."

"Yes, I know," she said. "That's why I came here."

"To purchase a Ming vase?" asked Mr Tanakas.

Everything was happening to him these days.

"Yes," said Miss Grobney. "Any dynasty will do. I don't hold for dynasties, do you? To me, a Ming vase is a Ming vase. May I see one?"

"But, madam, what makes you think that pet shops were instituted for the sale of Ming vases?" asked Mr Tanakas.

"Oh, I don't think they were instituted for that," Miss Grobney told him with a charming vague smile. "But, you see, Miss Kendall, a friend of mine, once found a Ming vase in a pet shop. By mistake it was being used as a water container for an Ibis.''

''Here,'' said Mr Tanakas, ''we make no such mistakes.''

''Oh, dear,'' said Miss Grobney. ''Well, since I'm here I just think I'll take an armadillo.''

Mr Tanakas wrung his hands.

''We happen to be out of armadillos,'' he said. ''Could I interest you in something else? A coatimundi, perhaps?''

''Oh, dear,'' said Miss Grobney, undecided. ''Are you *sure* you haven't a Ming vase?''

Clovis was fascinated by Miss Grobney. He wanted her for his own. Such charm! Such naïveté! It was certain that a woman like this would attract others like herself to her circle. If only Clovis could get into that home. What a chance to study the species *homo sapiens* at first hand, on its own home grounds.

''Pretty lady,'' said Clovis in his most charming voice. ''Oh, see the pretty lady.''

Miss Grobney turned toward him and smiled.

''Why, I do believe I'll take a parrot,'' she said.

She walked over to the cage.

''My, he's pretty,'' she said. She turned to Mr Tanakas. ''That is, I *hope* it's a he,'' she said. ''I've always wanted to own a boy-parrot.''

At this moment Clovis' regard for her knew no bounds.

''Of course it's a boy-parrot,'' said Mr Tanakas, anxious to get rid of Clovis.

''How do you know?'' asked Miss Grobney shrewdly. ''Somewhere I seem to have heard—''

"Me, Clovis," said Clovis promptly. "Pretty Clovis. Clovis wants a cracker, a crack-crack-CRACKER! Take a look at him. Whew!"

So Miss Grobney purchased Clovis and took him home to live with her.

n the way to the Grobney residence in a taxi-cab, Clovis gave himself some good counsel.

"If you are going to study human beings in their own habitat," he told himself, "you must not let them guess your secret. If they learn that you can think and talk and remember and repeat, they'll become inhibited. You must not let the bugs on the slide suspect the scientist behind the microscope."

Clovis had not yet decided exactly what he was going to do with the knowledge he intended to acquire. Perhaps he'd write a book or else lecture at Harvard.

The Grobney home was almost but not quite a mansion. It was dignified, its architecture old-fashioned but graceful. It was evident that Miss Grobney was wealthy. They were met at the door by Beamish, the butler. Beamish was a small, white-haired person who, despite his age, was as spry as a cricket.

"Ah," he said as he took Clovis' cage, "Miss Caress has brought us a parrot. How delightful to be employed in this home. Always surprises."

He led Miss Grobney into the parlor and put the parrot cage on a small table.

"Now," he said, "I shall go prepare tea."

He went on, humming happily to himself.

It seemed that Beamish had spread the news in other quarters, for soon Miss Grobney's sister, Lulu, and her brother-in-law, Sylvian Prent, came into the room. They, too, were small and white-haired and, like Miss Grobney, their complexions were the smooth pink-and-white of Dresden china.

"Oh, dear Caress," Lulu said of her sister. "A parrot. How original of you. Whatever made you think of it?"

"Well," said Caress Grobney, "I really intended to get another Ming vase but the man didn't have an armadillo and so, well, here he is. His name's Clovis."

"You know something?" said Sylvian. "I was getting a little bored with Ming vases. After the first hundred or so they seem somehow to lose their savor. Really, Caress, I must compliment you. A parrot is indeed an innovation."

"Oh dear," sighed Miss Grobney. "I am so happy that you approve."

"We always approve of what you do," said Sylvian. "You know that. Does he talk?"

"Whew! Whew!" said Clovis. "Pretty polly. Take a look at him. Wow!"

"Oh goodie," gasped Lulu. "He really does talk. And the conceit of him. "Take a look at him." Fancy that."

They all laughed merrily and then Beamish entered, wheeling a tea table.

"Oh dear," said Miss Grobney. "I really don't believe I shall take tea today. You know how I am whenever I'm extravagant-whenever I buy a Ming vase or something I always deny myself some luxury to balance things. This time I think I shall go without tea.''

''We quite understand,'' said Sylvian.

''That way I don't feel so much like the idle rich,'' Miss Grobney further explained. She went to her room and Beamish also departed.

''She'll probably gorge herself on chocolates,'' smiled Lulu indulgently.

''I daresay,'' agreed Sylvian. ''But let her enjoy herself. She has such little time for this world.''

''Don't we all?'' asked Lulu.

''That's right,'' assented Sylvian. ''Life is so ephemeral.''

''How true,'' said Lulu. ''Pass the jam, please.''

Sylvian passed the jam.

''That's why I don't hold with people who pretend a horror of murder,'' he said. ''As a matter of fact, I do not agree with the term murder at all. If life were everlasting and one deprived one's fellow man of that boon, then I'd agree that murder would be the correct word to describe the act. Pass the milk, darling.''

Lulu passed the milk and Sylvian continued his discourse, a discourse which Clovis found to be more and more disconcerting.

''But inasmuch as the days of man are numbered, I do not believe that killing him constitutes murder,'' Sylvian said. ''I maintain that it is a mere matter of subtraction. You have not deprived him of anything that he was not destined to lose anyway. You have merely moved up the date.''

"How succinctly you put it," said Lulu admiringly. "These biscuits are lovely, aren't they?"

"Delicious," agreed Sylvian. "Now you take the case of Nero. He killed his mother. But has history any right to judge him as a murderer? If he had not killed his parent would she be alive today? Would her bones be any the less dust? Can it possibly make any difference to her now that the inevitable was a trifle premature?"

"Of course not," declared Lulu. "Oh, how comforting you are, dear Sylvian. How fortunate to have known you and married you and grown old with you."

"It was not only a physical union but a marriage of minds," said Sylvian. "It is I who am fortunate."

They clasped hands and gazed tenderly into one another's eyes, their tea forgotten.

Beamish entered and smiled indulgently.

"At it again," he said. "The honeymoon never has ended, has it?"

"No, indeed," agreed Sylvian. "How unfortunate, Beamish, that you never entered into the placid, happy state of matrimony."

"If I had seen Miss Lulu first," said Beamish gallantly, "I would have done so. But as it is, I must be content with warming myself in the glow of your happiness."

He wheeled the tea table out and Lulu and Sylvian followed him, hand in hand.

Clovis was a little dazed. Never in all his studies had he run across such a philosophy. It was contrary to all human morality. And to think that it came from such mild-mannered, gentle people as Sylvian and Lulu! Clovis tried to convince himself that what he had heard was merely conversation and that there was no conviction behind it. Then he remembered the passing reference to the paucity of Miss Grobney's days and a slight chill ran up his spine. Certainly these humans would be worth studying, especially from the vantage point of a parrot, supposedly unthinking and uncomprehending in his cage.

Clovis' reflections were interrupted by the silent arrival of a girl who floated into the room like a pale shadow—a white-skinned, golden-haired bit of perfection. Never, outside of the Red-Head in the jungle, had Clovis seen anything so beautiful.

"Hello, Clovis," she said in a voice like running water. "Aunt Caress told me about you. I think you're beautiful. My name's Honeybird."

Clovis wanted to tell her how aptly he thought she had been named. He wanted to tell her how beautiful he thought she was but he had his part to play in this household and he could not deviate from it.

"Ark, ark, ark," he squawked. "Take a look at him."

"Oh, you funny bird," said Honeybird, "you almost made me laugh. That's lovely of you to almost have made me laugh, dear Clovis. I am so unhappy. I could tell you so many things about me."

Clovis was quivering to hear anything about Honeybird, no matter how inconsequential, but he dared not ask.

"How fortunate you are to be a parrot," sighed Honeybird. "Just to be pretty and dumb and unthinking. To have no hopes and no worries and no ambitions. Just to exist and be happy. Look at me, Clovis. *I'm* pretty, too, aren't I? Look at my lovely white skin, my breasts—they're white, too, Clovis—my legs. Ah, my lovely legs. But it's all a sham, Clovis, a hollow mockery. You see, Clovis, my pretty dumb Clovis, I am merely a flower without perfume.''

She sighed again and wafted herself out of the room.

It was late at night and all was quiet in the Grobney household. Clovis was having a disturbed dream. Usually his dreams were dull but this one suffered from bad casting. In it, Honeybird and Red-Head were inextricably mixed up. Their component parts seemed interchangeable. At times Honeybird had the brilliant plumage of Red-Head and she raced Clovis through miles of space. And then Red-Head had Honeybird's face and golden hair and she, too, soared through the blue with Clovis. Finally he awakened.

Sad, haunting thoughts ran through his mind. He felt strange and alone in this household. There was the intangible, barely suggested evil of the two little Prents. There was the intoxicating nearness of Honeybird. Then, mixed with that, was memory of Red-Head and even August. Clovis wondered what August, poor, stupid, well-educated August was doing. He felt out of place all of a sudden.

"After all, is this wise?" he asked himself aloud. "Could it be that your destiny lies not in this direction but whence you came? Alas, who can answer?"

"It's a cinch *I* can't," said a voice from the darkness. "I'm all screwed up myself."

The lights went on. Standing in the doorway was a tall, dark-haired, slightly handsome young man. He weaved cautiously toward Clovis and breathed alcoholic fumes at him.

"What's biting you, chum?" he asked.

"It was purely a personal problem," snapped Clovis, who was allergic to the odor of intoxicants.

"Well, don't get shirty about it," said the young man. "You're the one who brought the matter up. I've got troubles enough of my own without taking on the bellyaches of a parrot."

He observed Clovis more closely.

"Say, you really were talking, weren't you?" he asked. "Making sense, too. Now I've got it. You're drunk."

"I am not," declared Clovis. "I never drink."

"Then *I'm* drunk," said the young man. "I'm beautifully, gorgeously, deliriously accordion-pleated. I've never had a jag like you before."

"I'm not a jag," Clovis told him. "Your ears aren't deceiving you. I *am* conversing with you. But if you happen to remember the occurrence in the morning, which I doubt that you will, nobody'll believe you and I won't back you up."

"Don't worry," said the young man. "I won't tell anybody. Not in this household. They don't like me."

He wept for a few moments, then wiped his eyes.

"My name's Grover Grobney," he said. "I'm a distant relative, cousin or something. I'm the black sheep of the family."

63

"I can see why," Clovis told him.

"Don't pass it off so lightly," said Grover. "It's no small thing to be the black sheep of *this* family. It's an accomplishment and it takes constant application."

"That's one thing I've noticed about you humans," said Clovis. "You tend to flaunt your vices like banners in the breeze. Think how really great your accomplishments might be if you faced life with a clear head."

"If I had a clear head I wouldn't be seeing you," said Grover, "and I wouldn't miss that for anything."

"The inability to face reality is as much of an alcoholic curse as the invention of non-existent fauna," said Clovis. "Right now your senses are blurred. Alcohol courses through the fine membranes of your brain. The tender lining of your stomach is being corroded."

"I," said Grover, "have a cast-iron stomach."

"That's what *you* think," said Clovis. "In reality, the lining of your stomach is as sensitive as the membranes of your eye. Would you put alcohol in your eye?"

"No," admitted Grover. "But I put hot soup in my stomach and I wouldn't put that in my eye either. How do you account for that?"

"You're dissembling," said Clovis, crossly.

"You know, you're too good to keep all to one's self," Grover said. "It isn't vouchsafed for one man to get this drunk very often. I think I'm going to share you with my pals."

"More drunkards?" asked Clovis.

"Oh, no," said Grover. "A bunch of stuffed shirts. They used to run around with me and they couldn't keep up with me. So they formed a club as protection against me. They call it the Anti-Alcohol-and-Grover-Grobney Society. They formed it right after a little party I threw for them last New Year's Eve.''

''An admirable idea,'' declared Clovis.

''Let's go show you to 'em,'' suggested Grover.

''Decidedly not,'' said Clovis. ''I'm no freak to be demonstrated in club houses.''

''Who said you were a freak?'' demanded Grover. ''You're a horrible example. When they see you it'll strengthen them in their determination to lay off the grog. God knows, if I see enough of you I might take the veil myself.''

This speech reactivated Clovis' crusading spirit. He decided to investigate this commendable Anti-Alcohol-and-Grover-Grobney movement. Perhaps that was why his life had been spared in the jungle. It could be that, instead of leading ungrateful parrots to a finer way of living, he was intended to assist humankind to fight off the dreadful effects of alcohol.

''I'll go,'' he said finally. ''I think I shall enjoy communion with your former associates.''

Grover placed Clovis on his shoulder and they took a cab to a mid-town spot. As they started up the steps to the brownstone building, a formidable looking doorman appeared.

''No you don't, Grover Grobney,'' he said menacingly. ''You don't come in here. The gentlemen are having a quiet evening of cribbage.''

''I just want to introduce a friend to ''em,'' said Grover placatingly.

"You haven't got a friend," said the doorman. "And if you do have one he ain't with you. You're all alone and you're drunk."

Clovis, having decided to investigate the Anti-Alcohol-and-Grover-Grobney Society, was not to be thwarted by a mere doorman.

"How about me?" he asked.

"You don't count," said the doorman. "You're just a parrot."

Then he stared at Clovis.

"Quit goggling at me, you anthropoid," snapped Clovis.

Then he called upon all that he had read in the way of obscenity and added to it all that he had heard aboard the steamer. He started out by cursing the doorman in a sort of Portuguese patois fancied by the Canary Islanders, switched to a bastard Polynesian, made a neat transition into polyglot Arabic and wound up by abusing him in the purest Celtic.

"Holy Mother," gasped the doorman and hit the sidewalk without having made use of the intervening steps. He headed in the general direction of the George Washington Bridge with long, easy strides calculated both for distance and endurance.

Without further molestation, Clovis and Grover proceeded into the clubroom. A group of young men were sedately playing cribbage and drinking milk. They were painfully bored.

"Hi, fellows," called Grover.

A young man looked up.

"Hi, Grover," he said and then looked again. "What're *you* doing here, Grover?" he asked.

"Yes," said another young man. "We told the doorman to shoot to kill if you so much as entered the block."

"I think you're going to have to get a new doorman," said Grover pleasantly.

Another young man looked up from his cards.

"Hey, fellows," he cried. "Rally around. Here's Grover."

Others approached and stood in an unfriendly circle.

"It's Grover, all right," said one. "The one that cost me the only girl I ever loved."

"The one that broke me up with my wife and children," said another.

"The one who caused me to lose my job with the Manhattan Trust Company," said a third.

"The merry Andrew who bought me a drink in a bar on Forty-Second Street and three weeks later we woke up as able-bodied seamen aboard a Greek freighter," said a fourth. "When I returned, my sainted mother threw me downstairs and my dog bit me."

"We don't like you, Grover," others chimed in. "Go away, Grover."

"Gee," said Grover, his eyes brimming, "it's swell to be back with the old gang again."

"Don't pull that, Grover," said one of the young men. "We're immune to you, Grover."

Clovis noticed that every time they said 'Grover' it sounded like an epithet.

"I'm not trying to tempt you, fellows, really," protested Grover. "I'm not the kind of lush that tries to lead others on. What I say is, if a man wants to be on the wagon then let him be on the wagon."

"Then what *are* you doing here, Grover?" asked one of the men. "Especially with that silly-looking parrot on your shoulder."

"That's right," said another. "He *has* got a parrot on his shoulder, hasn't he? I didn't notice it before."

"That's why I came here," said Grover. "This here parrot's enough to make a fellow not only give up drinking but eating as well. That is, if you can see him. Can you?"

They surprised Grover by assuring him that they could see Clovis.

"What is there about the parrot?" asked one.

"He talks," said Grover.

"All parrots talk," said a young man.

"Not like this parrot does," said Grover. "He's a god-damned blue nose. A moralist. Name of Clovis."

"Oh, come off it," a man scoffed. "Parrots haven't got any morals."

"I'll measure mine against yours any day," snapped Clovis angrily.

"Did you hear that?" gasped the man addressed.

"No," said another hastily.

"Neither did I," added a third.

"A typical example of mass hypnosis," declared Clovis, "only in reverse. You face something you cannot comprehend and you try to delude yourselves into the belief that it does not exist."

There was a moment of silence and then one of the men addressed Grover in a cold, angry voice.

"If you *must* get drunk and come here with a parrot on your shoulder, why did you have to pick such a pedantic parrot? Why not just an ordinary parrot that'd say "Polly wanna cracker,'' and maybe bite your finger if you got too near it?''

''If it'll make you happy,'' said Clovis, now thoroughly aroused, ''come a little closer and *I'll* bite your finger.''

''I'll bet he would, too,'' said a voice.

''Come, come,'' said Clovis, his temper cooling as he remembered his mission, ''all this will get us nowhere. I come here not to quarrel with you but to study your noble movement. Perhaps with my great knowledge I can assist you in expanding your campaign against the enemy, alcohol.''

''He's inviting himself right in, isn't he?'' said a man.

''He sure is,'' said another. ''What do you know about our enemy, alcohol, Clovis?''

''Tell 'em that one about the lining of the stomach and the eye,'' urged Grover. He turned to the others. ''You won't believe this,'' he assured them.

Clovis repeated what he had said to Grover earlier in the evening. The others stared incredulously at him.

''Howling horntoads,'' said one. ''Did you ever hear anything like that as an argument against drinking?''

''Not even from my sainted mother,'' said another. ''And *she*, not being very bright, used to figure out some dillies.''

''Go on, Clovis,'' said a man. ''Tell us some more.''

Aflame with evangelical zeal, Clovis told them everything he had ever read or thought up about the evils of drink. He told them how one's first sip of alcohol lubricated the downward path. He explained the effect of the beverage on one's internal organs, how it blurred the vision, slowed up the reflexes, retarded metabolism, hardened the arteries, and played hob with the liver. He gave his best efforts to his dissertation on the moral aspect of drinking; how it weakened the will, killed ambition and inevitably led to a state of destitution and degradation.

After he had finished, Clovis preened his feathers a little.

"Obviously they are impressed," he told himself. "Perhaps, at last, I have found the justification for my existence—to revive and lead the great prohibition movement."

Finally the gloomy silence was broken by one of the younger men.

"Good God," he said. "This fantastic fowl claims that, in spirit, he is one of us. If he's right, what does that make us?"

"It makes me shudder," said another.

"The kind of weaklings who'd give up drinking just to pamper our livers," said a third.

"Not only that," someone pointed out, "but it seems we've dedicated ourselves to some sort of loathsome crusade to save the kidneys of our fellow-men."

"An invasion of privacy of the worst sort," declared another. "Not only indelicate but indecent."

"Do you mean," asked a young man, "that our society is supposed to stand for what that parrot just said, all that drool?"

"*He* seems to think so," came the answer.

"Including that obscenity about the alcohol in your eye?" asked a fast weakening member.

"Seems as though," he was told.

"Well, I'm glad I found out," said the man. "I only intended to remain a member until my ulcers cleared up anyway."

"The thing that appealed to me was that Grover Grobney couldn't join," a fellow member declared.

"Yes," said another, "I thought it was worth staying on the wagon for a while, just to get away from Grover."

"And how we have maligned Grover," a member said. "If it had not been for him we never would have seen ourselves in our true light. If it hadn't been for him and his parrot we might have persisted in our course. Who knows but what the movement might have spread as this puerile fowl predicted. We might have become the instruments through which nature's noblest gift to mankind might one day be denied us."

"Yes," said another man. "Good old Grover. There he stands, not preoccupied with his internal organs, not concerned with his neighbour's kidneys, but in a normal state, gloriously drunk. Ossified."

"Thank you," said Grover. "I try to do my best."

"Hold on," said Clovis. "The intent of my remarks seems to have escaped you. My purpose was not to show Grover's inebriation in a praiseworthy light. It was to—"

"Shut up, Clovis," said a member. "We've heard quite enough from you, Clovis."

"Enough to last a lifetime," agreed another member. "Be so kind as to drop dead, Clovis."

"God, how I need a drink," somebody moaned.

The meeting of the Anti-Alcohol-and-Grover-Grobney Society wound up in a bar where everyone became extremely intoxicated, even Clovis. At first they had to pry Clovis' beak apart to pour the liquor down him but, after the third slug, he began demanding his share of the libations. Finally, he was leading them in the singing of the old English song which had so shocked Miss Ewbanks.

Eventually the police arrived and herded most of the membership into patrol wagons. Grover and Clovis escaped after Clovis cursed a partolman in such angry ancient Hebraic that that good officer went straight to the precinct station and turned in his badge.

Clovis rode home in a taxicab with Grover, feeling a little like an African missionary who had just partaken of a choice portion of roast young girl a bit on the rare side.

"My intentions were good," he told himself fuzzily. "My intentions are always good, but something always happens. What evil spirit is it that seems intent upon preventing me from achieving my destiny?" And he burped.

He drowsed off, wishing he had not guzzled that last Martini.

*C*lovis awakened to a whirring sound the next morning. He was pleased finally to learn that the sound came from a lawn mower being pushed across the grass outside and not from his brain cells running amok, as he at first suspected.

Miss Grobney, followed by the Prents, entered the parlor. They fussed about the cage for a while, trying to get Clovis to talk. He did not feel in the mood and the most they could elicit from him was a belch.

Grover came downstairs carrying two suitcases.

"Why, Grover," said Miss Grobney, "wherever on earth are you going?"

"Away," said Grover "I have stood too much. When you attempted to cure my drinking by hiding the bottles, that was fair enough. It tested my ingenuity. When you started putting curative powders in my coffee, that was part of the game. It was science against my determination to drink myself to death. Up to that point there was a certain element of sportsmanship in what you did. But when you set a parrot on me, especially a mealy-mouthed hypocrite of a parrot like Clovis, then I draw the line."

"What on earth did Clovis do to you?" asked Miss Grobney.

"Plenty," said Grover. "It's too harrowing to relate. All I intend to say is that Clovis is a hypocrite of the first water and I advise you to keep an eye on him. He's a drunkard."

"Nonsense," said Lulu Prent. "All this is something you imagined during a period of alcoholic excess."

"Perhaps it was," admitted Grover, "but that bird was behind it all. There's not room beneath this roof for the both of us. I am leaving."

"But what do you propose to do?" asked Miss Grobney.

"I propose to spend the rest of my life blackening the name of Grobney," said Grover and made his departure.

"I don't think he can do it," observed Sylvian Prent.

"You don't think he can do what?" asked Miss Grobney.

"Blacken the Grobney name," said Sylvian. "Least-wise, I don't think he can blacken it any more than your brother did."

"Well," said Miss Grobney, "he's young and he seems pretty determined. You can't tell."

"That'll be fun, won't it?" asked Lulu. "I mean, watching for his name in the crime news and things like that?"

"Won't it, though?" agreed Miss Grobney. "Remind me to subscribe to the *Mirror*, will you?"

"What's that whirring sound?" asked Sylvian.

"It seems to be the lawn mower," said Lulu.

"It must be the new gardener," said Miss Grobney.

"It must be," said Sylvian. "The other gardener refused to mow the lawn—said it weakened the roots and encouraged dandelions."

"Let's go watch," suggested Miss Grobney eagerly.

And the three rushed happily out the front door.

Clovis was feeling badly about Grover.

"Again fate is against me," he said unhappily. "I tried to reform him and now he's out blackening the name of Grobney."

Presently there were footsteps and a man came in, his face hidden by the huge bunch of flowers he carried.

"It must be the new gardener," Clovs decided.

The man placed the flowers on a table and turned. Clovis gasped. It was Thaddeus Campo.

"Hello, Baby," said Thad. "Didn't think I'd find you, did you? Well, it was simple. I just went to all the pet shops. By the way, what did you do to Mr Tanakas? He's got his place up for sale."

"Never mind that," said Clovis. "What are you up to?"

"Oh," said Thad, "I'll keep this job as gardener until the time comes when I can safely steal you and put you to work for me."

"If you try, I'll make so much noise the police will come," threatened Clovis.

"I'll figure a way around that," Thad told him. "In the meantime there's no hurry. I haven't yet decided just how to exploit you so's to get the most money out of you."

"I shan't co-operate," Clovis said.

"Remember the hot-foot," said Thad, and laughed evilly.

Honeybird floated into the room, humming softly to herself.

"Hello, Clovis darling," she said. "Do you like it here? Do you have enough to eat? Oh, Clovis, I *so* want you to be happy because then perhaps you'll make *me* happy."

Then she saw the six-foot, handsome Thad.

"Oh, Clovis," she said. "It's a man. A stranger. Who do you suppose he is, Clovis? I have never seen him before. It *so* disturbs me to see strange men, especially young ones."

"My name's Thad Campo," Thad said. "And I'm no stranger, I'm the gardener. Tell her that, Clovis."

"Tell him," said Honeybird to Clovis, "that my name's Honeybird and for him not to mind my ways. I'm shy, Clovis. Tell him that."

"Tell Honeybird that she needn't bother being shy," Thad said to Clovis. "Just tell her that my only interest in this household is to keep the garden in order."

He went out and Honeybird followed him at a distance. She followed him down the pathway to the rose garden and stood silently behind him while he started to prune the bushes.

"Do you love flowers?" she finally asked.

"Hate 'em," said Thad.

"Well," sighed Honeybird, "so do I, in a way. You see they remind me of myself. Born to be beautiful for a moment, only to waste away and die."

You planning on dying real soon?" Thad asked her.

"My death is a slow death," Honeybird explained. "It might go on and on for years and years."

"Fine," said Thad, "then I can get on with my work without having to worry about any bodies."

"To you," said Honeybird, "I look just like any normal girl, don't I?"

Thad gave her a brief glance.

"I wouldn't say that," he said. "You look a little off, if you ask me."

"Oh, how perceptive you are," said Honeybird. "I'm *more* than a bit off. You see, I'm a biological mess."

"Aside from being a little dippy," said Thad, "you look all right to me."

"That's just surface appearance," said Honeybird. "Underneath I'm cold and barren. Disinterested in the other sex."

"Inasmuch as I'm of the other sex and you're not interested in me, why don't you go away and be disinterested in somebody else?" demanded Thad.

"It happened in Los Angeles," said Honeybird dreamily. "The beaches were full of bronzed young men. I sat, gazing at them by the hour, and every time I did, a peculiar feeling came over me. At times I thought I was going to faint. This feeling persisted until I couldn't eat or sleep. I finally went to a doctor. His name was Haslett and—"

"I don't want to hear about it," said Thad.

"This doctor gave me many examinations. One examination consisted of—"

"Let's not go into details," begged Thad. "Have you no delicacy?"

"Not after what that doctor did to me," Honeybird told him. "Anyway, after it was all over, the doctor told me to go away and he'd write out a report and send it to me. He didn't have the heart to tell me about my affliction face to face."

"I wish you'd be as kind-hearted," said Thad. "I don't want to hear about your affliction either."

"It was glandular," went on Honeybird. "There were a lot of technical terms but I realized what they meant. They meant that I was not interested in the other sex and even if I was it'd do me no good. There could be no offspring."

"Why are you telling *me* all this?" asked Thad.

"So's you'll know what you're up against," said Honeybird, "in case you ever decide to try to force yourself upon me."

"I have no intention of trying to force myself upon you,"said Thad. "Will you please go away?"

"Even if you succeeded, even if you went as far as you possibly could go—*all* the way, I mean—"

"You've made yourself abundantly clear," said Thad. "Let's drop the subject."

"I would be utterly unresponsive, completely unaroused," said Honeybird.

"I'll take your word for it," Thad agreed.

"You don't have to take my word for it," declared Honeybird. "Would you like to try it and find out for sure? Now?"

"No," yelled Thad. "For God's sakes, no."

"Well," said Honeybird, "any time you're curious, any time you'd like to find out—"

And she floated gently away, her tiny feet seeming hardly to bend the blades of grass upon which she trod.

As the days slipped by, Clovis sat in his cage in the Grobney parlor and brooded. He was trying to find sense and shape in his existence. Every time he had attempted to give a meaning to his life, he had failed. His own kind had no use for him; the Indians saw in him only fuel for a sacrificial fire; his words of wisdom had had a reverse effect on Grover and his friends. Somewhere there must be fertile soil where his sage counsel would find root and flourish and blossom for the benefit of others. Or was wisdom a goal in itself; to be kept to one's self; not to be shared with the masses?

Clovis could not believe the latter. He was convinced that somewhere, somehow, he would find his mission. But, at the moment, he found it difficult to concentrate on the matter. A feeling of lassitude was coming over him. Not even the constant threat of Thad Campo seemed very real to him. He found it hard to respond in a half-way civil manner to the overtures of Miss Grobney and the two Prents. He was in a funk.

Only when Honeybird entered the room did he awaken. Then his pulse beat faster, a warm feeling came over him, and his thoughts, although jumbled and confused, were delightful.

"Oh, Clovis," she would say, "oh, dear, dumb, delightful Clovis. I do believe you understand me. You are the only friend I have, dear Clovis."

And the warm feeling would come over Clovis again and his head would spin.

One day Honeybird came to Clovis in a particularly depressed mood.

"Ah, Clovis," she said, "the world of my life has entered its final eclipse. The warmth of the sun is gone. My being is bathed in a cold light. The chill increases, Clovis. The light grows more and more dim. You see, my dear, there is no reason for my being. I am a flower that cannot attract the bee, the fruit which has no flavor. Ah, Clovis, not to be loved; not to be able to attract love; not to be able to love."

She shed a few tears and finally floated away from his vision. Clovis was touched. There was a lump in his throat.

"Ah," he said to himself, "how alike we are. She, too, seeks a reason for her existence. She, too, feels the loneliness of an unreceptive world. She, too, has a great need, a great void to be filled. Alas, if only I could be of assistance."

Then slowly and stealthily—like a thief in the night—a thought crept into Clovis' brain. What Honeybird needed was understanding. Yes, more than understanding: love. And so did Clovis. It was a delirious thought, a dizzy thought, but it took complete possession of him and he was powerless to dispute it.

Late that night he undid the latch of his cage, flew out an open window and soared to the window of Honeybird's bedroom. He perched behind some potted ferns where he could see her but she could not see him. She was weeping softly in her sleep. Her adorable cheeks were sprinkled with salt dew.

''You sleep, my love,'' said Clovis softly, ''you sleep but yet you do not sleep. Your mind is groping, seeking in a black void. It does not know its way. It is lost and the blackness stretches on forever.''

In her sleep, Honeybird uttered a plaintive, lonesome cry.

''But, ah, my love, somewhere there is light. Here there is light. It is a gentle light, a soft light, a warm light. It is the light of love. I love you, Honeybird.''

Honeybird stirred in her sleep and a faint smile caressed her lips.

''My adored one,'' said Clovis. ''Fear no more. Seek no more. My love will protect you. My love will guide you. My love will take you by the hand and lead you down sunny paths lined with blossoms. My love will be yours forever.It is a love that seeks nothing in return. It is a selfless love, yours to command. So sleep, my love, sleep and dream no more.''

Honeybird slept soundly, peacefully, a smile of contentment curving her lips. Clovis drank in the sight and then silently flew away. He was tempted to soar off into the night on the wings of his new happiness but he begrudged even a few minutes away from the house wherein his adored one slumbered.

The next morning, Beamish discovered the cage unlocked.

"No telling what mischief this bird might get into," he muttered, and went away.

He returned with a padlock and securely imprisoned Clovis. But Clovis was not dismayed. His thoughts were too full of the night before.

"At last," he told himself, "I have a purpose in living. To love her and guide her. To ask nothing for myself but to be her strong staff, her shield and her armor against unhappiness. Ah, what a blessing to be in love. Clovis, at last you have found the ultimate meaning of existence. All else is dross."

He looked out the window and down to the lawn where Thad Campo was puttering with some petunias.

Honeybird appeared on the lawn, as gay and beautiful as a new species of flower. She moved close to Thad and gazed adoringly at him.

"Well, what do you want?" he asked gruffly.

"Nothing, Thad," said Honeybird softly. "Nothing after last night."

"Nothing after *what* last night?" asked Thad.

"Don't pretend, Thad," said Honeybird. "Don't pretend that you don't remember."

"Remember what?" asked Thad.

"That you came to me," said Honeybird, "in my bedroom."

"I did no such goddamned thing," declared Thad, horrified.

"Yes, you did," insisted Honeybird. "If not in person, then in spirit. Your spirit called out to mine; it was in communion with mine. I heard your voice speaking to me, telling me not to be afraid."

''Well,'' said Thad, ''I don't know where my spirit was, but this body was in Bud's pool hall cleaning up a crap game. Does that spoil any illusions of romance?''

''You were inspiring,'' said Honeybird. ''You aroused me, Thad, how you aroused me!''

''The hell I did,'' said Thad. ''How?''

''Spiritually,'' said Honeybird. ''Not in a carnal sense but selflessly. You aroused me to my destiny. I have been seeking someone to love me. Now I realize that I should have been seeking someone to love.''

''Well, go seek him elsewhere,'' begged Thad. ''I'm not your man, believe me, Honeybird.'

''You may say that,'' said Honeybird, ''but all was revealed to me in our mysterious communion of souls last night. It is my fate and duty to love you and guide you and ask nothing in return for myself. My joy shall be in the giving. The true emotions which have been denied me, I shall simulate. Oh, Thad, how I shall simulate. Would you like to test my powers of simulation, darling? Just name the time. How about now?''

''Please, Honeybird,'' said Thad, ''you're sweet in your way. You're beautiful and—''

''You're just guessing,'' said Honeybird. ''You don't know how really beautiful I am. My breasts, my beautiful white thighs, my virgin, my barren—''

''Stop it,'' pleaded Thad in an agonised voice. ''I never want to hear that word again.''

''My whole beautiful body,'' went on Honeybird. ''It's all yours, to do with what you will, any place, any time. Now, for instance.''

"Look, Honeybird," said Thad earnestly. "You are upset. You had a dream and it's affected your mind. You don't know what you're saying or to whom. You don't even know me. I've got a shady past and a dubious future. Why not go give yourself to someone more worthy?"

"I don't care what you have been nor do I care what you intend to be," said Honeybird. "My love shall guide you. If you desire to be an artist, I shall be your model—in the nude—on the coldest days. If your ambition is to be a gangster, I shall be your moll. Would you like that, dear?"

"No," said Thad emphatically. Then, in an effort to get rid of her at any cost, he went on: "Let's not talk about it any more now. Let's resume the conversation another time, a few years from now when we both know our own minds. Run along, will you? I'm busy."

She went away reluctantly, looking back many times, turning the full glow of her inviting smile toward the unworthy Thad Campo.

On his perch at the window, Clovis was tasting the full flavor of spiritual quinine. Again in his quest for a shining goal, a light of inspiration, he had run into a blind alley, smack against a wall, and into the darkness of despair.

"The pure, the untainted, the selfless love I offered to her she has accepted and transferred to my enemy, Thad," he told himself. From the depths of his soul came bitter laughter. "The Cyrano of the birds," he said.

Oh, what an accursed fate to be a parrot!

Clovis spent the rest of the day in a coma that was akin to death. It was not until late that night that he became conscious of what was going on about him. Lulu and Sylvian Prent entered and sat cozily in front of the fireplace. They were silent for some time, watching the flicker of the flames.

"How lovely," Lulu finally murmured. "So peaceful. Just like our lives together."

"How true," said Sylvian. "It is dying down to a glow but there is still flame. The ashes have not yet conquered."

"A few more hours of warmth," said Lulu dreamily. "In our case a few more years of love. Did you get the cyanide?"

"Ah yes," said Sylvian. "Also some arsenic and strychnine. As an afterthought I also purchased some prussic acid."

"You think of everything, don't you?" said Lulu fondly.

"I try," said Sylvian modestly. "Still I haven't made up my mind just how to dispose of her. Poison isn't the only way, you know."

"Now it is coming out," said Clovis, his lethargy suddenly departing. "They are plotting a murder. How wise I was in not allowing them to know I can understand what they say."

"What else have you in mind?" inquired Lulu.

"Well," said Sylvian, "there are simple methods like smothering. Or there is the accidental fall in the bath-tub. Again there is the plain, uncomplicated clout on the head."

"I know," said Lulu, shivering a little. "But those things are uncomfortable. They hurt."

"Tush," said Sylvian indulgently. "Pain is so short-lived. Do you remember the pain of a tooth pulled during your childhood? Or leastwise, do you feel it *now* ?"

"I see what you mean," said Lulu. "You *are* so comforting, Sylvian."

As the conversation went on, Clovis was vaguely aware of a shadow. The shadow began to move, and finally in the flickering light of the fire, Clovis perceived that it was Beamish. Clovis was elated. He felt sure of Beamish's loyalty to Miss Grobney and he was confident that he could count on the servitor as a witness and an ally.

Beamish came closer and finally Lulu noticed him.

"Ah there, Beamish," she said. "What are you up to?"

"Nothing, Miss Lulu," said Beamish.

"Don't try to fool me," said Sylvian. "You were eaves-dropping."

"Well, I was a little," admitted Beamish.

"Naughty Beamish," said Lulu. "I'll wager you heard everything we said."

"Not everything," chuckled Beamish, "but I gathered that you're planning to do away with Miss Grobney soon."

"Oh, you clever-pie," said Lulu with mock petulance. "We intended it as a surprise."

"It's hard to surprise old Beamish," said Beamish proudly. "I've been suspecting something like this all along."

"I should have known," said Sylvian. "After all, you, as well as we, realize the urgent need for money."

"Ah yes," said Beamish. "The root of all evil."

"It's only evil if you haven't got it," Sylvian pointed out.

"Quite true," admitted Beamish. "Have you settled on the method of the—ah—extermination?"

"You mean the hastening of the devoutly to be wished eventuality," Sylvian corrected him. "Well, what would you suggest? I have assorted poisons."

"So I overheard," admitted Beamish. "But somehow I distrust poisons. It's devilishly hard to convince a coroner's jury that such potions were accidentally administered."

"There's truth in that," agreed Sylvian. "Carry on, Beamish."

"Well," said Beamish, "it seems to me a window would serve our purpose admirably. You see, people are always falling out of windows and there's no way of proving they were pushed."

"Excellent, excellent," said Sylvian. "Now how do we get her to a window?"

"Oh, it's simple," said Beamish. "The moon is out tonight. Just invite her to have a look at it."

"Oh, you indispensable Beamish," cried Lulu admiringly. "That's it, exactly."

"Incidentally I didn't know the moon was out to-night," said Sylvian. "I adore moonlight nights."

"We've got plenty of time," said Lulu. "Let's all go out and take a look at it."

They went out and Clovis was left alone. Spiritually he had staged a great comeback. From feeling totally inadequate and unwanted, he had rebounded to a sense of his own importance, to a realization of the great need that existed for his peculiar endowments.

"It is not such a curse to be a parrot," he told himself. "Especially an intelligent one. If I had not been a parrot they would not have talked near me and I would not have been in a position to save Miss Grobney's life."

Then he began to ponder a method of putting his intention into effect. Since he could not go to Miss Grobney, he reasoned, then he must bring her to him.

He began to squawk loudly, to whistle shrilly, being careful not to be too articulate lest the three conspirators become suspicious of his secret. Finally his strategy bore fruit. Miss Grobney came hurriedly into the room.

"Gracious, Clovis," she said. "Whatever on earth is the matter?"

"I was trying to attract your attention," said Clovis in a conspiratorial whisper.

"Well, you succeeded," said Miss Grobney. "Incidentally, since you were making so much racket a while ago, why are you whispering now?"

"Sh-h-h," said Clovis softly. "You are in danger."

"Gracious," said Miss Grobney. "Am I really?"

"They plan to push you out a window," whispered Clovis. "Tonight."

''Who plans to push me out a window?'' asked Miss Grobney?''

''The Prents,'' said Clovis. ''Lulu and Sylvian. Beamish is in on it, too.''

''Heavens,'' said Miss Grobney. ''How do you know all this?''

''Although it does not seem to surprise you in any way,'' said Clovis, ''I am a highly intelligent parrot. I can understand and remember and repeat everything I hear. I overheard the Prents and Beamish plotting against your life tonight.''

''How do you know it was me they were plotting to kill?'' asked Miss Grobney.

''It was obvious,'' said Clovis. ''And anyway Beamish brought the whole thing out into the open by referring to the victim as 'Miss Grobney.' ''

''Oh dear,'' said Miss Grobney. ''How unfortunate. How unfortunate, indeed. You see, Clovis, Beamish never refers to me as 'Miss Grobney.' He always calls me 'Miss Caress.' ''

''What are you trying to tell me?'' asked Clovis apprehensively.

''My niece, Honeybird, is also a Grobney,'' said the little old lady. ''Beamish always refers to her as 'Miss Grobney.' ''

''Then you mean it is she?'' said Clovis.

''Of course,'' said Miss Grobney. ''We were planning to kill Honeybird for her money. How unfortunate that you found out.''

She went to the window.

''Lulu, Sylvian, Beamish,'' she called. ''Come here, please. Hurry.''

Miss Grobney came back and spoke mildly to Clovis.

"You see," she said, "my brother, for some reason, perhaps it was because he hated me, left all his money to Honeybird. Now do you understand why it became necessary for us to kill her?"

"No," said Clovis.

"Dear me," said Miss Grobney, "if you are as clever as you say you are, you should understand. Honeybird has all the money and *we* need it. Isn't that simple?"

"It's monstrous," declared Clovis.

"It's monstrous, indeed," agreed Miss Grobney. "There are four of us and only one of her. Why, do you know that that wilful child won't even *divide* with us? In cash, I mean."

"You seem to have been living well," Clovis pointed out. "This house is positively cluttered with Ming vases."

"That's just it," said Miss Grobney. "The child is supporting us. She gives us everything we want. Her generosity is positively humiliating."

"What's humiliating about it?" asked Clovis, striving to gain a point from which he could argue with all his brilliance and save Honeybird's life.

"Why one can't buy Ming vases with another's money," Miss Grobney pointed out. "It just isn't done. We want the fun of spending our own money after we kill Honeybird."

Lulu, Sylvian and Beamish entered, inquiring as to the trouble.

"Oh dear," said Miss Grobney, "Clovis here seems to be an extraordinary, gifted parrot. He not only can understand what is said within his hearing but he remembers it and can repeat it. In addition to that he has moral scruples.''

''Meaning that he is aware of our little plans for Honey-bird?'' asked Sylvian.

''Yes,'' answered Miss Grobney. ''At first he thought it was me you were going to kill.''

''How could he?'' said Lulu. ''We all love you so. And besides *you* have no money.''

''Well, well,'' said Sylvian, ''it seems that Clovis presents rather a serious problem.''

Again Clovis felt an arrogant sense of power. Once more his faith in himself was restored. After all it *did* pay to be an intelligent parrot. He, he felt, had these people at his mercy.

''It may be,'' he said, ''that I shall agree not to reveal this foul scheme to Honeybird. That depends on whether you are willing to give me your solemn oaths that you'll immediately vacate these premises and never again molest that beautiful creature in any manner whatsoever.''

''Oh nonsense,'' said Miss Grobney. ''We wouldn't think of making any such promise, and if we did, we wouldn't keep it.''

''Then what do you propose to do?'' asked Clovis, still feeling that he had the whip hand.

''Well,'' sighed Sylvian, ''I suppose we'll just have to kill you.''

Clovis was shocked. It hadn't occurred to him that *he* was in danger.

''Kill me?'' he echoed. ''But that'd be murder.''

''Dear, dear,'' said Sylvian. ''Murder. How loosely they're using that term these days. My dear Clovis, you are a mere parrot. One cannot be hanged for exterminating a bird. The worst that could happen to us would be a slight unpleasantness with the Humane Society."

He went to the fireplace and began selecting a poker.

"Dearie me," said Miss Grobney. "He was such a pretty bird and he cost a hundred dollars."

"Well, that's what he gets for being an eavesdropper and a tattletale," said Lulu.

"Ah," thought Clovis, "so at last I die. My good intentions misunderstood, my noble motives thwarted. And what will be my epitaph? Eavesdropper! Tattletale! Ah, you deceased Von Lerners perceive the result of your labors."

As Sylvian returned with the poker, Thaddeus Campo stepped in through the open window, a baseball bat in his hand.

"I've heard everything," he said. "And this is where you all get off. I saw this parrot first and he happens to be valuable to me. There'll be no killing, unless—"

He glanced meaningly at Clovis.

"Clovis," he said, "do you think you could manage to see eye to eye with me on a few commercial enterprises I have in mind?"

Clovis was tempted to put up a final argument in favor of his ideals, his professional ethics, but death was too imminent and life was too sweet for such quibbling.

"As you wish," he said.

Honeybird had slipped silently into the room.

"I heard noises," she said. "What is the matter? Why do you threaten my folks with a baseball bat, Thad? Not that I'd think of denying you the pleasure, if it be a pleasure. I'm just curious."

"They have been hatching up a plot to kill you for your money," Thad explained.

"Were you?" Honeybird asked her folks.

"Yes, dear," said Miss Grobney. "*You* know why."

"All that money," said Lulu. "That beautiful money."

"I think you're detestable," said Honeybird, "all of you."

"Well," asked Thad, "what do I do now? Shall I turn 'em over to the police?"

"Don't be naïve, my dear boy," said Sylvian pleasantly. "Do you think the police would take the word of a gardener and a parrot against ours? And if you're counting on Honeybird, don't. Can you imagine a jury taking her seriously, with all her talk about glands and such?"

This latter remark impressed Thad. He was undecided.

"Oh, let's not bother with the police," said Honeybird. "Just let them go. Let them pack their things and go away. I never want to see them again."

"We'll go," agreed Sylvian, "but not far and you'll see us again, take my word for that. We're not giving up quite so easily, my darling."

"All that money," said Lulu as the four elderly persons marched out. "All that beautiful money."

"Oh dear," said Miss Grobney at the door, "I feel so sorry for you, my darling Honeybird. Listen for us at night, dear. You'll hear our footsteps on the grass. You'll hear our voices in the wind. Wherever you go you'll feel us near you."

And then they were gone.

Honeybird dismissed them from her mind. She turned to Thad, her eyes shining.

"And now that you have saved my life, what are you going to do with it?" she inquired. "Ask of me what you will, no matter how preposterous—anything!"

"I don't want anything," said Thad. "I'm giving your life back to you. May it be long and prosperous and happy. Bless you. Come on, Clovis."

He picked up the cage and departed, while Honeybird crumpled on to a sofa and sobbed like a grievously wounded child.

had and Clovis had settled in a small apartment uptown.

"I've rented an abandoned beer hall on Broadway," Thad told Clovis. "I'm having the signs painted and the place decorated in a jungle motif. We'll open in two days and you'll knock 'em dead."

"I hope I do," said Clovis. "I hope I literally knock them dead. You, too."

"Oh, don't take it so hard," Thaddeus said. "All you have to do is deliver a short lecture four or five times a day and the money'll come rolling in."

"Never before have I felt any need of money," said Clovis.

"You're going to feel the need of it from here on," said Thad, "or else you won't eat."

"It's humiliating for a philosopher to have to earn his living," declared Clovis. "If Socrates were alive today, would they exhibit him in a beer hall?"

"You're no Socrates," Thad told him. "You're just a parrot who's too smart for his britches. And remember they fed Socrates hemlock."

"I would prefer hemlock to being exhibited to the ignorant masses," said Clovis. "How long shall I have to put up with this before you release me from my promise?"

"Let's see," said Thad, "I've saved your life twice. How much do you think it's worth?"

"Very little," said Clovis bitterly. "I am a failure, a discredited scientist, a mountebank philosopher, a—"

There was a timid knock at the door and Thad opened it to admit Honeybird.

"Now what?" asked Thad.

"Oh, Thad," said Honeybird, "I couldn't stay in my house any longer."

"Why not?" asked Thad.

"Miss Grobney and the Prents and Beamish," said Honeybird. "They're all over the place. Remember what she said? About hearing footsteps on the grass? Well, I heard them, ever so soft and menacing. I heard their voices, too. Always they came from the next room. When I went into that room they were gone and I could hear them whispering and giggling from the next."

"That's just your imagination," declared Thad. "You'd better go back home."

"Oh no, not for anything in the world," shuddered Honeybird. "They'd never let me rest. One day they'd kill me. Please don't make me go back, Thad."

"Well you can't stay here," said Thad. "As you can see, there's only one bed."

"I won't take up much room," said Honeybird. "If you insist I'll always stay on my own side. I won't do anything you don't want me to. But I'll do *anything* you want me to. Of course, as the doctor said, I'll be cold and unresponsive but I'll try not to let you know it. I'll simulate, Thad. I'll simulate like anything.''

"No," said Thad, "it just won't work."

"How do you know?" asked Honeybird. "How do you know it won't work until you give me a chance to simulate?''

"I wasn't talking about simulating," snapped Thad. "I was talking about your living here with me. Although I may be as lowdown and depraved as Clovis thinks I am, I have some sense of sportsmanship if not decency. You'll have to go.''

"Oh, if you're thinking of my name," said Honeybird, "just forget all about it. I was expelled from five boarding schools before I was fourteen and on my fifteenth birthday—''

"I don't want to hear about it," said Thad.

"And if it's the cost of my upkeep you're thinking of—I don't eat much and, in the second place, I've got scads of money. You can have any part of it.''

"I don't want your money," Thad told her.

"Oh, you don't have to take it all," said Honeybird. "How about just a little bit of it? Would you like a million to start with, dear Thad?''

"No," said Thad.

"You're quite willing to degrade me for money," said Clovis. "Why do you balk at accepting this girl's generous offer?''

"It's a matter of perverted principles," said Thad. "We Campos will do almost anything for money but we balk at taking it from a woman. No, Honeybird, you keep your money and leave me alone to make my living in my own dishonest way."

"I'll help you, then," said Honeybird. "I'll lock up my old money and we'll go out together and rob people. I'll be your moll."

"I don't need any moll to exhibit Clovis," Thad said. "It's the most legitimate scheme I ever thought up."

"Well, maybe we can teach Clovis to steal," suggested Honeybird. "He ought to make a splendid jewel thief. You know, flying in and out of windows?"

"Isn't it enough that Thad proposes to make a mountebank of me?" demanded Clovis. "Must *you* make me a common crook?"

"You'd be a very uncommon crook," declared Honeybird. "You'd do it for me, wouldn't you, Clovis? Dear Clovis?"

"No," said Clovis, "I wouldn't."

"In that case," said Honeybird, "I'd singe off all your feathers—with a blow torch."

Clovis shuddered. And this was the damsel for whom he had poured out all his love just a few nights ago. Well, he was glad he was over that. The softer emotions were no longer for him.

"What's this mania you have for larceny?" he asked. "Why should you be so preoccupied with crime when you are so wealthy?"

"I'd do anything to please Thad," said Honeybird. "*Anything.*"

"Nobody asked you to do anything for me," said Thad. "Especially is it unnecessary for you to become my moll. I don't want a moll."

"All right," agreed Honeybird. "That's up to you. You can have me for anything you want me for."

"Which brings us back to the starting point," said Thad. "All I want you to do for me is to go away."

"They'll kill me," whimpered Honeybird.

"Then go a long way away," said Thad. "Spend some of your money on guards. Hire yourself a castle with a moat around it."

Honeybird looked toward a window and her face went white.

"Look," she said and pointed.

Framed in the window was the beaming face of Miss Grobney. She smiled benignly, waved her hand and was gone. Thad ran to the window and threw it open. All was blackness. Miss Grobney was nowhere in sight. As Thad turned away from the window, a piece of paper slid beneath the door to the hallway.

Thad picked up the piece of paper. It read: "You can't help her. She's doomed unless she listens to reason and gives us that beautiful money."

Thad threw open the door and looked down the hall. He saw the Prents and Beamish disappearing down a stairway. A silvery laugh floated tauntingly back to him. He felt a rash of goose pimples breaking out all over him.

"Lordy," he thought belatedly, "we're on the third floor. How did Miss Grobney get to the window? And how did she disappear so fast?"

He went back into the room, trying to conceal his true emotions.

"I don't think they really intend to harm you," he told

Honeybird, ''but I don't suppose it'll hurt if you stay here where I can keep an eye on you.''

''You won't be disappointed,'' breathed Honeybird. ''My skin, my—''

''And cut that out,'' snapped Thad.

Later that evening Honeybird began to yawn.

''Shall we go to bed?'' she asked. ''Before we're too sleepy?''

Thad went into the bathroom to undress. When he came back, Honeybird was in bed—exactly in the middle of it.

''You take either side you want,'' she said. ''It doesn't make any difference to me.''

Thad got an extra blanket, wrapped himself in it and settled into a chair.

''Is that where we're going to sleep?'' asked Honeybird. ''My, I don't think there's room for both of us.''

''There isn't,'' declared Thad. ''Go to sleep.''

He turned out the light and there was a long silence.

''Thad?'' came Honeybird's voice.

''Yes?'' grumbled Thad.

''Thad?'' she repeated. ''Why are you sleeping in that chair?''

''Because I *like* sleeping in chairs,'' snapped Thad.

Another long silence.

Then the soft voice came again. ''Thad?''

''*Now* what do you want?'' asked Thad crossly.

''Did you really want me to go home?'' she asked.

''No, I suppose I didn't,'' admitted Thad from the darkness.

He was almost asleep when she spoke again.

"Thad?"

"Yes?" he said drowsily.

"Thad," she said, "do you love me, just a little?"

"Of course I do, goddam it!" he exploded. "Else why do you think I'm sleeping in this confounded chair?"

She sighed happily and went to sleep.

"It seems," said Clovis to himself, "that one cannot trust human beings even in their depravity. Here this man insists on appearing to be above moral scruples and yet, in some respects, he is the soul of honor. I wonder if he really would have given me the hot-foot?"

Clovis dropped off to sleep after having decided that Thad really would have.

It was the day of Clovis' degradation. In a gaudily decorated room, full of faked jungle atmosphere, he sat on a gilded perch behind a velvet rope. Outside Thad was ballyhooing what he called, "The wonder of the age. The world's greatest attraction. Clovis, the Omniscient."

A few idlers paid quarters and drifted into the room. They stared disappointedly at Clovis.

"It's only a boid," said one.

"What did you expect?" asked Clovis. "Didn't you know that a parrot is a bird?"

"Well," said the man, "we expected a bigger bird, something terrific. What's there about *you* worth a quarter?"

"I deliver lectures," said Clovis. "Name your subject."

"Who wants to hear a lecture?" asked a small boy.

"Do you tell fortunes?" asked a woman hopefully.

"Of course not," said Clovis. "You should be old enough to know that fortune-tellers are frauds."

"That's what you think," snapped the woman. "One told my sister she was going to die and my sister died."

"I can predict the same thing for you," said Clovis, "and I'm no fortune-teller."

"When?" demanded the woman. "Tell me that."

"I don't know," replied Clovis.

"See?" said the woman. "He admits he's a fake."

"I am not a fake," declared Clovis. "I just don't pretend to be a fortune-teller."

"Then what *are* you?" asked a fat man. "Do you sing?"

"I am not an entertainer," said Clovis. "I am a lecturer."

"Out in the park," said the small boy, "we can hear all the lectures we want for free. Why should we pay a quarter to hear *you* lecture?"

"I wouldn't know," replied Clovis. "As far as I'm concerned I wish you'd keep your quarters. I wish that I had never met any of you."

"Now he's insulting us," said the fat man.

"Obviously, the whole thing's a fake," declared a thin man, entering the circle around Clovis.

"That's what I said," declared the woman. "He can't even tell fortunes."

"That isn't the point," explained the man. "This parrot appears to be talking logically. He appears to understand what we say and to be able to answer us."

"And I don't like his answers," said the fat man. "He's too fresh."

"That's what proves he's a fake," said the thin man. "The very fact that he seems to understand you and talk back to you demonstrates that. No parrot can do those things."

"This one can," said the fat man, pointing. "He told me he wished he'd never met me. I guess my quarter's as good as anyone else's."

"But, my dear man," said the thin man, "you insist on thinking that the parrot is doing the talking. Obviously, it is a clever ventriloquist doing the talking."

"Don't be a jerk," scoffed the fat man. "There ain't a ventriloquist that good."

"And there *ain't* a parrot who can do what this parrot seems to be doing," said the thin man angrily.

"What do you mean, *seems* to be doing," demanded the fat man. "Ain't I got eyes and ears?"

"Yes, but no brains," snapped the thin man.

"He's got more brains than *you* have," said the irritated Clovis. "You're one of those wise guys with just enough intelligence to suspect trickery in everything."

"Who's a wise guy?" demanded the thin man.

"*You* are," replied Clovis.

"If I didn't know you were a fake, I'd knock your block off," said the thin man.

"You sure told him off," said the fat man, now on Clovis' side.

"When's the show going to start?" demanded the small boy. "Do you do card tricks?"

"No I don't," said Clovis. "This exhibition is purely educational. Would you like to hear a lecture on evolution?"

"What's that?" asked the boy.

"It's about the origin of species. In other words, it tells you where you came from," said Clovis.

"Where do you think I been all my life?" leered the small boy. 'I *know* where I came from."

Clovis launched into his talk and his audience, at first, listened apathetically. Then they began to grow interested but not from an educational standpoint. Soon there were angry murmurs and their faces grew hostile.

''I'm not going to stand here and listen to a parrot tell me my grandmother was a monkey,'' declared a woman suddenly. ''It's an outrage.''

''I didn't say your grandmother was a monkey,'' explained Clovis. ''I said your remote ancestors.''

''Well, you can't make it remote enough not to be an insult,'' insisted the woman. ''The Good Book says—''

''Evolution can be reconciled with the Good Book,'' declared Clovis. ''It says—''

''And I'll not stand here and hear a parrot quote the Good Book,'' said the woman. ''It's blasphemy.''

''In your case,'' said Clovis, ''I seem to have made a mistake in so far as evolution is concerned.''

''I accept the apology,'' said the woman.

''Definitely your ancestors were not monkeys,'' declared Clovis, ''but if you keep at it and breed carefully there's a slight chance that some day one of your descendants will turn out to be a monkey.''

''Did you hear what he said to me?'' demanded the woman. ''Is there no gentleman in the crowd?''

''Good lord!'' breathed a small man. ''I hope that bird *is* a fake. It'd be awful if a mere parrot could think up things like that.''

''He's thinking 'em up,'' said the fat man. ''And he's no mere parrot.''

''Whatever kind of a parrot he is,'' said a prosperous-looking man, ''he's a Communist, I can tell you that.''

"You talk just like a goddamned Fascist," snarled a poorly clad little man. "That bird's a reactionary."

"Or whoever's doing the talking for him is," said the thin man.

"Who's doing the talking for *you*?" snapped Clovis. "And where did you dredge up such ignorance?"

"That's it," declared the thin man. "The old familiar pattern. You don't agree with a Communist and you're ignorant."

"What kind of an argument is that?" asked the shabby man. "Of course you're ignorant. You look like you came from a long line of dopes."

"The pattern again," said the thin man. "Name calling's part of it."

"Whyn't you call him a name right back?" suggested the small boy, seeing a chance of getting his quarter's worth out of the affair. "This is a free country."

"I couldn't think of anything descriptive enough to call him," said the thin man.

"I could," said Clovis.

"Say," said the shabby man, "whose side are you on?"

"I'm against all of you," declared Clovis. "You nauseate me."

"Spoken like a Communist," declared the prosperous man. "He's against all of us."

"The Fascist line, if I ever heard it," said the shabby man.

"What's all this blather about lines?" demanded the woman who had earlier tangled with Clovis. "This here lousy parrot insulted me. Aren't any of you jerks gonna protect a woman's good name?"

"Jerks, is it?" snarled the fat man. "What kind of language is *that* to go with a good name? It's always the same. Gentlemen get into a friendly philosophical discussion and along comes a woman injecting personalities into it. Incidentally, I'll bet your name's no better than it should be."

"And me a grandmother," gasped the woman, and she slapped him.

"Here's something for your grandchildren," said the fat man, and slapped her right back.

"Since when do you go around slugging ladies?" asked a burly stevedore.

"I never hit a lady in my life," said the fat man. "Any dame that whaps *me* in the puss isn't a lady, she's a tomato."

"And *this* is Mother's Day," said the recently slapped woman.

"What of it?" demanded the fat man.

"You got something to say against Mother's Day, perhaps?" asked the stevedore.

"Why not?" asked the fat man. "Some of the goddamndest floozies I ever saw were mothers."

The stevedore shuddered in the face of this blasphemy and then slugged the fat man. The riot was on. Soon fits were flying all over the place, blood was spouting, and the small boy felt that never in his life had he spent a quarter so judiciously. All too soon for his liking, the police arrived and quelled the disturbance by laying about them with their clubs.

Finally, the room was cleared of all excepting Clovis, Thad Campo and a police lieutenant.

"What kind of heinekabooberie's going on around here?" demanded the lieutenant.

"I was running an educational show," said Thad. "Somebody started a riot."

"What kind of an educational show?" asked the lieutenant.

"Clovis, here," said Thad, "was delivering a lecture."

"Oh, the parrot was?" said the lieutenant. "And his name's Clovis, eh? What was the lecture about? Crackers?"

"No," said Clovis. "Evolution."

"Indeed," said the lieutenant. "And what do you know about evolution?"

"Shall I tell you?" asked Clovis.

"No, I guess you'd better not," said the lieutenant. "It doesn't make much difference, anyway. The main thing is that you were inciting to riot."

"The people incited themselves to riot," declared Clovis. "In the final analysis, they forgot all about me and started pelting one another with their intolerances."

"If there'd been no lecture there'd been no riot," said the lieutenant.

"I was exercising my rights of free speech," insisted Clovis. "Is that illegal?"

"Look," said the lieutenant, "in my book anyone's got the right to free speech as long as nobody disagrees with him. After that it isn't free any more, it's liable to cost you a bat on the noggin. I don't know what you said and I don't care. All I know is that what you said caused a riot and that puts you in the wrong."

"What kind of philosophy is that?" demanded Clovis.

"Cop's philosophy," said the lieutenant. "Now I could take you two down to the precinct station but I'd rather not. The captain's got ulcers and he's never learned, as I have, to take things for granted. He's liable to ask me how come a parrot can give out with all the guff you're dispensing and I just wouldn't care to try to answer him. After I see the last of you I'm going to forget all about you. I won't even mention you to my wife."

He turned to Thad.

"You'd better close this joint up," he said. "And then you'd better take this disciple of Darwin and tie a brick to his neck and sink him in the Hudson. I've seen good men beaten half to death for exercising their rights to free speech. How far do you think you're going to get with a parrot?"

With that he left them.

had, Clovis and Honeybird were gathered together in the small apartment.

"It grows increasingly obvious," declared Clovis, "that there is no place for me in your civilization. Your people have not learned to dissociate wisdom and talent from its source. The fact that I am a parrot, instead of increasing the import of what I have to say, lessens its effect. I am either laughed at, ignored, scorned or put down as a fraud. I am not even a successful mountebank."

"It's all my fault," declared Thad. "I guess I've got a lot to learn about showmanship. There must be some way of presenting you so's Broadway'll sit up and take notice."

"If you ask me," said Honeybird, "you're barking up the wrong alley. You ought to go to Los Angeles. You'd be surprised at what they'll pay money for out there."

"There's too much competition in Los Angeles," declared Thad. "I'm going to stick it out on Broadway."

"We are doomed to failure," said Clovis, who was feeling sorry for himself. "I am the wrong kind of an anomaly. If I were a human being who talked and thought like a parrot, perhaps you could exhibit me in a sideshow.

110

But, being a parrot who thinks and talks like a man, I am an implausibility which human beings cannot comprehend and, failing to comprehend, refuse to take seriously."

"It seems to me," said Honeybird, "that all this talk boils down to money and it's a waste of time. I've got plenty of money. Why don't we all go out and spend it? Preferably in an orgy."

"I've explained that," said Thad firmly. "I can't and won't take your money."

"Why not?" inquired Honeybird.

"Because, like all of us," said Thad, "I have my weaknesses, else I'd be a more successful crook than I am. I have an Achilles heel on both feet. The right one concerns my vanity. Whatever I am or hope to be I want to be solely through my own efforts."

"And I know what's on the left foot," declared Honeybird. "You just won't take *anything* from me. No matter how many times I explain I won't miss it a teensie-weensie bit."

"I thought we'd settled all that," said Thad.

"How can it ever be settled?" asked Honeybird. "Inasmuch as we can *never* be married—"

"We could be married today," said Thad, "if it weren't for your money."

"Not in my condition," Honeybird told him. "I'm soil where no seed will grow. I'm a flower without—"

She broke off suddenly in a listening attitude.

"What's that peculiar noise?" she asked.

"What noise?" asked Thad.

"It's a ticking noise," said Clovis. "I've been conscious of it for some time."

111

"It's an awfully loud clock," declared Honeybird.

"We haven't got a clock," said Thad. "Only our wrist watches."

Suddenly the ticking seemed to become ominously more loud and clear. Thad began a systematic search. Tantalizingly the sound seemed to come from all quarters of the apartment. After having overturned the bed, ripped out all the bureau drawers and emptied the cupboard, Thad found the source. It was the oven of the kitchen stove.

He threw open the oven and exposed a cleverly contrived time bomb operated by an alarm clock. He ripped the wires from the lethal machine and wiped cold beads of perspiration from his brow.

"Look," said Honeybird, "there's a note."

Thad read the note.

"Greetings," it said. "If you find this you'll not be so lucky the next time. If you don't find it we'll soon have our beautiful money."

"That settles it," said Thad. "We're going to Los Angeles."

They pointed Thad's car west and drove for several miles in silence.

"Whew," said Thad, still shaken. "That fearful foursome! You know, I'd rather have all of the old Capone mob after me than those little geezers."

"Don't worry," said Honeybird, cuddling up to him. "I won't let them hurt you."

"It's you I'm thinking of," Thad told her.

'It's nice to have you thinking of me," sighed Honeybird. "If you'd only think along the right lines."

Four nights out of New York a huge truck began following Thad's car on a down grade. As Thad accelerated, so did the truck. He drove at a dangerously reckless speed but still the truck gained. Just as a crash seemed inevitable, Thad managed to swerve far enough off the road to lessen the collision to a side-swipe and reduce his damage to a smashed fender.

As the offending truck roared away in the distance a silvery laugh floated back. It sounded very much like Miss Grobney's.

That night in a motel, tired, cold and frightened, Honeybird crept like a kitten to Thad's side. It may have been simulation, but Thad lost his left Achilles heel.

*A*fter much searching and some bribery, Thad finally rented a three-room motel suite on Ventura Boulevard in the San Fernando Valley of Los Angeles. It consisted of two bedrooms and a kitchen, one of the bedrooms doubling during the daytime as a sitting-room.

Honeybird eyed the second bedroom with disfavor.

"You are *so* inconsistent," she told Thad.

Thad rubbed his hands together and turned to Clovis, who roosted on a bedpost.

"I've been thinking about your future all across the United States," he said, "and now I've got it all figured out. I'm going to get you in the movies."

"Oh, no, not that," begged Clovis.

"Listen," said Thad. "You want to be known, don't you? You want to be paid attention to, don't you? You've got messages, haven't you?"

"Yes," admitted Clovis.

"Then you've got to attract attention," declared Thad. "You need publicity. You need a propaganda outlet. There is no greater medium of propaganda than the silver screen. Properly directed it represents a force for good or

114

evil greater than all other media combined. Clark Gable appears in a picture without an undershirt and the undershirt industry goes into a tailspin. Louise Albritton endorses a soap and within a week thousands of young females are washing their faces instead of camouflaging them with cosmetics. Rod Cameron flies an airplane and Bob Paige—"

"I am not interested in airplanes, soap or undershirts," declared Clovis.

"That's just a superficial indication of the power of motion pictures," declared Thad. "Why, they're being used to popularize everything from Shakespeare to Salvarsan. Their potential greatness is demonstrated by the organizations which exist solely to harry and harass them and tell them what they can and cannot do. So jealous are various factions of their power that only the brave among them dare to speak a good word for a great president unless he has been dead long enough so's not to influence any current political trend. As a result of these pressure groups, the industry has created and sold a never-never land wherein babies are found beneath cabbage leaves. There are no politics and sin does not exist except in pale tones and even then the sinner is invariably punished. It is a world God never made and wouldn't approve of, but it bears the purity seal of the Johnson office. They need you, Clovis."

"You're speaking out of character and your vehemence only convinces me you are trying to sell me a bill of goods," remarked Clovis. "But there is something in what you say and you may, at last, have pointed me toward my destiny."

Thad, Clovis and Honeybird loaded into Thad's car and they launched themselves into the stream of Los Angeles traffic. The traffic signs plainly prohibited a speed of more than twenty-five miles an hour, so Thad drove forty miles an hour. A car, doing at least sixty miles an hour, came up behind them and struck them in the rear. The driver of the second car leaned out and bellowed at them.

"What in the hell were you doing parked in the middle of the street, you goddamned hick?" he demanded.

Clovis cursed back at him for some length and wound up by inviting him to get out and fight like a man.

"Ha," said the driver, "wouldn't I look silly out in the middle of Ventura Boulevard fighting a parrot?"

He backed his car a few feet, then pulled up even with Thad.

"It's a good thing *you* didn't say that," he said and drove on.

Thad piloted the damaged car to the studio where he had managed to wangle an interview. As they left the parking lot and started to cross the street, a huge sightseeing bus bore down upon them, honked its horn, skidded its tires and missed them by inches.

As the bus rolled on, there was a silvery laugh. Sitting on the top deck of the bus were Miss Grobney, the Prents and Beamish, waving merrily and as carefree as grigs.

With a chill of apprehension, Thad piloted the others in for the interview. The producer to whom they had been assigned was a jovial, bald-headed corpulent dignitary who had been untouched by any Hollywood scandal excepting that concerning his penchant for escorting other men's wives to horse races.

"What can I do for you?" he asked.

"It's what we can do for you," said Thad. "I'm offering you the opportunity of the age in the person of Clovis."

The producer stared appreciatively at Honeybird.

"What an odd name for a girl," he said.

"Her name's Honeybird," said Thad.

"That's an odd name, too," said the producer. "Who's Clovis, then?"

"I am," said Clovis.

"I see," said the producer. He turned to Thad. "What about Clovis?" he asked.

Thad gave the producer a brief but comprehensive resume of Clovis' antecedents, bringing him up to date.

"Interesting," murmured the producer. "Very interesting. Now what do you propose that we do with him?"

"Isn't it obvious?" gasped Thad. "Think what it would mean to have an educated, intelligent, eloquent parrot on the screen."

"I was thinking," said the producer. "And the answer is nothing. Do you by any chance think this bird would be a leading man? Would the women go for him like they do Walter Pidgeon?"

"Well," said Thad weakly.

"And if we put him on the screen as a freak, who would believe him? The customers'd think it was a dubbing trick, like making camels talk and I wish we'd never thought *that* one up. And as far as talking birds are concerned, Disney and Lantz and others've been making 'em talk for years and they're a darned sight funnier than Clovis could ever think of being.''

Thad's face fell, and the producer, being a kindly man, tried to relieve his obvious disapointment.

''What else can he do?'' he asked. ''Could he direct, perhaps?'' He stared at Thad. ''You don't think so, do you?'' he asked.

''No,'' said Thad unhappily.

''Could he write, then?'' asked the producer.

''Yes I could,'' spoke up Clovis.

''You have ideas?'' asked the producer.

''I've got a lot of ideas,'' declared Clovis.

''Name one,'' invited the producer.

''Well,'' said Clovis, ''they aren't concrete.''

''They never are,'' murmured the producer.

''They're messages, important ones,'' said Clovis.

''My,'' said the producer, closing his eyes, ''I can just see the crowds lining up in front of the New York Music Hall, stretching clear around the block. Traffic cops are out, the people are rioting.'' He opened his eyes and fixed them upon Clovis. ''Have you any stories to go with those messages, chum?'' he asked. ''A beginning and a middle and an end, stories that'd sustain interest and provide entertainment and sell tickets?''

''That will come later,'' Clovis told him.

''That's when you should have come to me, then,'' said the producer. ''Later.''

''You're just thinking of money,'' declared Clovis.

The producer turned to Thad.

''When you brought Clovis to me, what were *you* thinking of?'' he asked.

"Money," admitted Thad.

The producer turned to Clovis.

"Now that that's settled," he said, "suppose you go on. Tell me just what it is you think you have to offer the motion picture industry."

"I am educated," said Clovis.

"In the crap games on any set," said the producer, "you'll find more Phi Beta Kappa keys than dollar bills."

"I speak Greek fluently," declared Clovis.

"So does our bootblack," said the producer.

"I mean ancient, classic Greek," said Clovis.

"The Acropolis," said the producer, "hasn't been a first-run house for some time."

"You're deliberately misunderstanding me," declared Clovis. "I offer you the benefit of all the world's philosophies."

"We've got a research department that gives us the same thing," said the producer, "at fifty bucks per week per college graduate. Go on."

"I'd be wasting my time," sulked Clovis.

"I'm afraid we're both wasting our time," said the producer. "What this business needs, Clovis, is smarter people, not smarter parrots."

He stared appreciatively at Honeybird.

"We *might* be able to use you," he said. "Have you ever made a screen test?"

"I have nothing to offer you," Honeybird told him. "If you put me in a scene, a real love scene that required deep feeling and passion—I mean the ultimate in passion— I could only simulate. You see I'm a hollow shell, a flower without—"

"She isn't for sale," snapped Thad and took Honey-bird by the hand. "Come on, let's get out of here."

"On your way out," suggested the producer, "leave your phone number. Maybe some day we could use Clovis as an extra in a jungle scene. All he'd have to do would be to sit on a phony banana plant and flap his wings. He wouldn't even have to squawk. We'd dub *that* in."

They were again in the motel on Ventura Boulevard. Again Clovis' self-confidence was at low ebb.

"Alas," he said, "again I have failed. I see now that there is no place for me in the universe. Your people don't want me and my own people won't have me. Whither shall I go? What shall be my fate?"

"Oh, quit bellyaching," snapped Thad. "I'll figure something out yet."

"I know how you feel," declared Honeybird. "I know how it feels not to be wanted and even if you are wanted there is something within you—or something that *isn't* within you and—"

There was a knock at the door and in came Grover Grobney.

"Hi, Clovis," he said. "Hi, Honeybird." Then, to Thad: "I'm Grover Grobney, a sort of distant relative of Honeybird's. I know Clovis only too well."

"Glad to know you," said Thad. "Won't you sit down? Is there anything I can do for you?"

"Presently," said Grover. He turned to Clovis. "So

121

there you are, in person. I hate you, Clovis. God, how I hate you. Once I was a happy drunkard, but when I left home that day I was under the influence of a mastodonic mental upset. I couldn't decide whether or not you had really happened to me. Finally I decided that you had and I tried to drown you in grog. But it didn't work. Every time I lifted the glass of forgetfulness to my lips, I heard your nauseating voice saying: ''The lining of your stomach is as sensitive as the membranes of your eye,'' and I just couldn't swallow. Curse you, Clovis, you have made a teetotaller of me.''

''That's gratitude,'' said Clovis bitterly. ''However, I have come to expect nothing more from humankind.''

''How close a relative are you to me?'' asked Honeybird of Grover.

''I never stopped to figure it out,'' said Grover. ''All I know is we have the same name. Why?''

''I was wondering,'' said Honeybird, ''if you are sterile.''

''What a question,'' said Grover. ''Why do you ask?''

''Well,'' said Honeybird, ''I'm barren. I was wondering if it runs in the family.''

''Not too far back,'' said Grover, ''else we wouldn't be here.''

He turned to Thad.

''We don't know one another very well,'' he said, ''but we should. I'm afraid we've got a lot in common. Is there some place we could go and talk alone? I think I have something interesting to say to you.''

''Well,'' said Thad, ''we could get in the car and go somewhere.''

As Thad got his hat, Clovis gazed sardonically at Grover.

"When I last saw you, you threatened to go out into the world to blacken the Grobney family name," he said. "How are you doing?"

"Well, I'm a Hollywood agent," said Grover. "What do *you* think?"

He and Thad got into the car and drove to a cocktail bar.

"I like to spend as much time as possible in gin mills," explained Grover as they were seated. "I sit and wait for the divine urge to drink, but it never comes to me any more, thanks to that parrot. And speaking of Clovis, I understand you were trying to peddle him to a movie studio today."

"It was a flop," said Thad. "A complete bust."

"Well, I've been giving the matter considerable thought," said Grover. "And I've come to the conclusion that you're trying to sell Clovis in the wrong market. He isn't an entertainer. At heart he's a pompous, irritating little do-gooder, a reformer of the first and vilest water."

"That's true," said Thad. "Where do we go from there?"

"In this town," said Grover, "they sell many things. They sell climate and movies and oranges and flesh. They also sell the divine spirit."

"What?" asked Thad.

"They sell the divine spirit," said Grover, "in temples and groves and circus tents. They wrap it in a gaudy package and hawk it like bananas from the street corners. They cater to man's quest for immortality with a song and dance and a spurious promise. It is said that making motion pictures is the town's leading industry but I'll bet that the packaging and selling of phony religions is breathing on its neck.''

"Go on," urged Thad.

"It's a bastard offspring of show business and, as I say, it's outstripping its parent in the race for the shekels. Its apostles don't have to be ordained; they don't even have to be educated. All they need is an act that'll attract the poor and the sick and the weary and the discouraged and, having done that, to entertain, amuse and even frighten them a little; but above all to convince them that their participation in these shoddy blasphemies constitutes a communion with their Maker, a short cut to the promised land. On Sundays the air is desecrated with exhortations and howls and yelps and obscene bellowings and in the distance, if you listen, you'll hear the hornpipes of Hell.''

Thad shuddered.

"But there's money in it?" he asked.

"Scads," Grover told him. "And it isn't only the pennies of the poor that go to swell the coffers. Any time you can show a rich man a needle with an eye the size of the entrance to the coliseum, he'll pay a pretty penny for admission.''

"All this, I take it," said Thad, "concerns Clovis.''

"Of course," declared Grover. "I have a client who is fresh out of material. He needs a new act. He used to be one of the most prosperous peddlers of evangelical eye-wash in the business but the income tax people caught up with him and he got a two-year dip in the federal can.''

"You mean the people'd accept an ex-convict?" asked Thad.

''You don't know Los Angeles people,'' said Grover. ''They're indefatigable in their desire to submit like sheep to the celestial clippers. When one of their messiahs has a brush with the law and emerges two or three years later with a prison pallor, their hosannas are as joyful as if a tomb had been opened. You see, that's where the Devil comes in. He's not only handy for frightening one's followers but to blame one's own mishaps upon,'' continued Grover. ''Whenever one of these bezarks gets caught with the goods on him all he has to do is bawl loudly that the Devil planted it there. Whenever the cops arrest one of them for some thoughtless peccadillo with a sixteen-year-old girl, he has but to call them disciples of Old Nick and his temple will sell out to standing-room-only on the next Sabbath.''

''According to that, your client's eligible,'' commented Thad. ''Who is he and how come he's a client?''

''His name's Brother Christmas,'' said Grover, ''which proves that they'll stop at nothing. He happens to be a client because he has a yen for the radio, which industry has steadfastly rejected his services. He and Clovis ought to make a good team.''

''Just how?'' asked Thad eagerly.

''We'll depend a lot on Brother Christmas. He knows the ropes,'' said Grover. ''Offhand, though, I'd say we'll concoct some sort of esoteric cult with a lot of Oriental trimmings. The main attraction will be a sacred bird of prophecy. That's Clovis, of course.''

''I follow you,'' said Thad.

''He'll be something like a million years old and Brother Christmas will have discovered him, by divine direction, somewhere in Tibet or Outer Mongolia or some such goddamned place," said Grover. "He'll be a sensation. The yucks'll fall for him like snow in Skagway."

"Clovis," said Thad, "might boggle."

"Of course he'll boggle," admitted Grover. "But we'll win him around. He's more of a parrot than he thinks he is. He likes to hear himself talk. That and the fact that he'll be before the public eye and have a chance to justify his existence, as you quote him as wanting to do, will out-weigh whatever moral scruples he has left. Don't forget, when I met him, he first preached abstinence and then wound up drunk."

Grover watched as Thad downed his third bourbon and soda.

"Oh, for the divine urge to drink again," he said mournfully.

*C*lovis did boggle and not all the persuasion of Thad and Grover could sway him from his moral scruples.

Then they called in Brother Christmas. Brother Christmas was a tall, pale-faced man in his early forties. His voice was smooth and unctuous, his manner persuasive.

"Ah, Clovis," he said, "we understand one another, you and I. We are both philosophers. I am not as erudite as you, perhaps, but still we have the same goal. Another thing we have in common is that we both have been grievously misunderstood."

"At least I have," grudgingly admitted Clovis.

"To be misunderstood is the first cross we have to bear in this life," Brother Christmas told him. "But the goal is worth it, is it not?"

"What goal?" asked Clovis.

"To lift people above themselves, to give them a glimpse of glory, to give purpose and direction to their confused existence, ease their pain, and soothe their spirits; to give them a little of knowledge and guide them toward higher things. That is *your* goal, is it not?"

"It was," admitted Clovis.

"I can tell that it still is," said Brother Christmas. "I am certain that you will see the wisdom of my plans, once you understand them. You are quoted as objecting to the device of a million-year-old bird of prophecy."

"I am quoted correctly," said Clovis.

"But, to help the masses," said Brother Christmas, "you must first gain their interest. You must give them a little of mysticism in order to focus their attention on the more important things you have to say. Now this bird you will represent, just in spirit, of course, is merely symbolic of greater truths. True, you are not a million years old, but your philosophy is. True I did not find you in Tibet, but I found part of your philosophy there. Do you begin to understand?"

"Yes," said Clovis, now interested. "Go on."

"And as for the lectures you will deliver," said Brother Christmas, "they must, of necessity, be on the optimistic side. The people have so much woe that you must promise them a great deal of joy in order to lift their spirits from their present sodden state. If you promise them great happiness and thereby you give them even a little happiness, shall you have hurt them? Of course not. Oh, Brother Clovis, believe me. I understand these people. My only wish is, through you, to help them."

He went on and on, his voice smooth and purring, and soon he had Clovis almost in a state of hypnosis. He appealed cleverly to Clovis' vanity, praised him, cajoled him and, above all, held up to him the long-sought opportunity to fulfil his destiny. At last, Clovis had ceased to boggle. He was sold.

128

"Now, at last," he said, "I know why an obscure fate caused the Von Lerners to breed parrots for intelligence. Here, in Los Angeles, I have found a reason for my existence."

At the doorway, Brother Christmas shook hands with Thad and Grover, and he winked.

"How'd I do, brothers?" he asked.

"You did fine," said Grover, "and don't call me 'brother,' you unctuous sonofabitch!"

o they gilded Clovis' plumage and launched him upon the gullible salvation seekers of Los Angeles as 'Clovis, The Golden Bird of Prophecy.'

Attired in resplendent golden robes, Brother Christmas stood before a packed tabernacle and thundered forth the introduction.

"Hello, my beloved people," he bellowed. "Are you glad to see me?"

There were a few polite assents which did not please Brother Christmas.

"Then say it as if you meant it," he demanded. "Let the whole world hear you. Let that old Devil, skulking down in the sulphur pits of hell, hear you. Say it. Say: 'Welcome Brother Christmas.' "

"*Welcome Brother Christmas*," they roared, and having made such a racket, began to feel that the sentiment was sincere.

"Ah, indeed, you should welcome me," said Brother Christmas. "Not for my humble person—I am a mere creature of flesh and blood, even as you. My welcome should be for the great thing I bring with me. But before we unveil this precious gift, allow me first to tell you of how it was obtained for you. Many of you—I suppose *most* of you—think I have been in prison, don't you?''

There was an uneasy silence and Brother Christmas went on:

''Ah, how often have I exhorted you not to believe what you read in the newspapers? How often have I told you that the Devil is a publisher? Do you think that, as clever as he is, it is difficult for him to get his lies into print? When I received my great call, the Devil saw his opportunity. He tried to make you believe that I had committed a crime, that I was in durance vile. Why did the Devil go to all that trouble to discredit one lone mortal? I'll tell you why. He knew my mission. He was afraid. He sought to poison your minds so that you would not believe my great revelation.

''But I could not remain here to defend myself against the Devil. I had received a call from the Great Spirit and I obeyed. The call led me across thousands of miles of stormy ocean, thousands of miles of trackless wastes. It led me into danger and suffering and often I despaired of my life, for the Devil was on the job. Oh, I know he was here working against me, but the Devil can be two places at once, he can be many places at once, and I, being a mere mortal, could be only one place at a time. I rose to the Devil's challenge. I fought him with the power of the Great Spirit and I won.''

Brother Christmas paused and wiped his streaming brow.

''I won,'' he repeated. ''I was led finally to consecrated ground, to hallowed ground, to ground that had been held sacred by the mystics of Ancient Tibet. And there it was given unto me to perceive in person, Clovis, the Golden Bird of Prophecy. Ah, what a dazzling sight. I fell down on my knees and wept and thanked the Great Spirit for having conferred this great honor on me."

He let this sink in for a moment and then went on.

"And, who is Clovis?" he asked. "What is Clovis? Clovis is the sacred receptacle of the wisdom of the ages. He is the vessel which contains the answer to all the problems of mankind. And why was a bird chosen for such a trust? Only the Great Spirit in his inscrutable wisdom can answer. The lamb has been used as a symbol, why not a bird? I only know that it was vouchsafed to me to bring to you—Clovis."

At his signal, Thad and Grover, attired in less resplendent robes than Brother Christmas, unveiled Clovis. Clovis was an impressive sight, sitting on an elaborately carved throne, his feathers sending forth golden gleams.

There was a gasp of pleased amazement from the crowd. This was something. It was a new wrinkle. The parishioners felt grateful to be members of Brother Christmas' cult. How dull, they thought, how dull, indeed, is the Sunday of the Methodists.

Clovis waited for an impressive moment and then began to speak in a well modulated voice.

"When Brother Christmas refers to me as the receptacle of the wisdom of the ages," he said, "he means it as if he were referring to a book of philosophy. When he mentioned his travels and trials and tribulations, he was speaking allegorically. He meant the trials and the tribulations of the spirit. To achieve wisdom all of us have to suffer in one manner or another. But what is wisdom? That, my friends, shall be my next text for today."

Clovis launched into a long and boring sermon on what he conceived to be wisdom. Brother Christmas signalled frantically to him but Clovis ignored him. Finally, he realized that he was losing his audience. They were beginning to fidget, to whisper to one another, to stare vacantly at the ceiling. He stopped in mid-sentence.

"They're not listening," he told himself. "Is this failure again? Is my destiny again to elude me?"

For a moment he felt like abandoning the project and then his temper flared up.

"Listen, you fools, you dolts, you nincompoops," he screamed. "Am I to waste precious words of wisdom while you chatter, while you slither and scrape and pick your noses?"

"Oh boy," whispered Thad to Grover. "Here goes the old ball game. And in the first innings, too."

"I don't know about that," said Grover. "Listen."

"If I bore you, go home," yelled Clovis. "I do not propose to sit here and try to pound the sands of knowledge into the rat-holes of your mind unless you have the courtesy to listen. My time is too precious to waste on you, you alley-born sons of the gutter."

The crowd was electrified. Never before had they heard such delightful near-cussing. That they were being abused was of no importance. They were used to abuse. In fact, it impressed them.

"No, no," they shouted. "Stay, Clovis, stay."

They began to applaud and stamp their feet and whistle, their only way of demonstrating approval of what had gone on before and of expressing their desire for more of the same. Clovis felt a warm glow. Now, at last, he had them. He felt a gratifying surge of power.

"Nice going," whispered Brother Christmas. "Now that they're listening, give them the main dish. Remember what I said. Their great need is hope."

Clovis chided them for a while, then began to talk soothingly.

"There is nothing you cannot accomplish with knowledge and well disciplined minds," he told them. "It is obvious that the condition of most of you could be improved. Besides things of the spirit, there are material benefits for those who will listen. There is no reason why you should not have better homes, better automobiles, more food and more money."

Now they began to prick up their ears in earnest. This was what they'd been waiting for. Clovis noticed this, and so great was his satisfaction at commanding their undivided attention that he made promises more rash than he had contemplated. But the more glowing the promises became, the more attentive the audience became. They did not understand a great deal of what Clovis said but they got what they wanted out of the address. In its simplest terms, what they gathered from Clovis' remarks was that they were going to be shown a flower-strewn short cut to a financial Garden of Eden.

And then came the collection and this did not seem at all incongruous to the disciples of the newly born cult. They saw nothing outlandish in an economy which was going to make them rich by extorting from them the dregs of their purses. To them, their religion was a slot machine into which they patiently fed their nickels in anticipation of a gigantic jackpot.

The crowd dispersed happily, optimistically. There was a spring to their step, a backward tilt to their shoulders, animation in their conversation. There were few sceptics and these were quickly silenced.

''What do you mean the bird's a fake? We saw him, didn't we? We heard him talk. Remember what Brother Christmas said about the lamb? Why not a bird?'' And more of the same.

Thad and Grover mingled with the crowd and took in the remarks.

''Lord almighty,'' said Grover happily. ''Here, in Los Angeles, we have found the only people in the world who will accept philosophy from a parrot.''

Thad wasn't listening. Mingling with the happy congregation were Miss Grobney, the Prents and Beamish, their apple cheeks aglow with life and health. They saw Thad and waved gaily but there was a look in their eyes that made him shudder.

*A*fter the third week the tabernacle became too small to contain the crowds which came to hear Clovis. A large auditorium was leased and named 'The Temple of the Golden Bird.' This, too, was filled to capacity. Among the shabbily clad multitudes there began to appear some mink coats and, among these, many who had come to scoff remained to worship.

Clovis, after his many disappointments, had arrived at last. His cup was full, yea, running over. He loved these people of Los Angeles. They understood him; they respected him; they listened to him and followed him. That this feeling grew closer and closer to fanatical worship did not embarrass Clovis in the least. His ego grew enormously and he considered that worship was but simple tribute to his greatness.

To Clovis, appreciation and approval had become as the wine of life and to elicit more of it he learned to tell the people more and more of what they wanted to hear. His promises became more and more lavish and although they were, as yet, unfulfilled, they were answered by a continuous flow of cash into the collection plates.

Although Clovis did not realize it, Brother Christmas was guiding the whole project. Thad and Grover were content to accept their share of the boodle and let the gold mine operate without interference from them.

Thad and Honeybird moved into an expensive apartment where they lived in outward sin and inward discontent. Honeybird steadfastly refused to enter into a marriage that promised for her nothing but unceasing 'barrenness.' She was, on the other hand, quite willing to make the outward appearance of their existence more of an actuality. But, after that experience in the motel, Thad had remained faithful to his principles. Their discontent was not lessened by the frequent reappearance of Miss Grobney and her retinue. There were no more attempts on Honeybird's life but wherever she and Thad went they were sure to catch a glimpse of the four merry little grigs who waved to them pleasantly and grew more and more frightening because of the intangibility of their menace.

Brother Christmas was a good judge of timing. When it appeared that unsupported promises were failing in their drawing power at the temple, he organised his congregation along political lines and started a "Two Thousand Dollars a Year For Everybody Club." This did not mean that everybody was to be given the chance to earn two thousand dollars a year; it meant that everybody was to be given two thousand dollars a year as a bonus for merely existing. The congregation circulated petitions, threatened and browbeat politicians and finally got their fantastic scheme on the ballot.

Brother Christmas knew as well as most informed persons that the bill had no remote possibility of being voted into effect. But his followers and the followers of Clovis thoroughly believed in its possibilities. They *wanted* to believe. It was a shining light in their drab lives, its promotion kept them busy and out of mischief, and it kept them temporarily loyal to the temple. In addition to that it loosed their purse strings even more. Why quibble at the donation of a few dollars when soon two thousand dollars a year were to be theirs?

The new movement spread throughout the state. Soon Clovis was making speeches in San Diego, Bakersfield, Fresno and as far north as Sacramento. San Francisco gave him a cool greeting and he never went back there any more.

As the enterprise flourished and grew, Brother Christmas, who was obsessed with a desire for personal political power, made another move. Subtly at first, and through pamphlets of which Clovis had no knowledge, he began sowing seeds he had long nurtured for such an occasion. It seemed that not everybody was worthy of membership in the Temple of the Golden Bird. Some were unworthy even of membership in the commonwealth. These unwanted persons promptly quit the congregation but they made room for increasing hordes of new members.

Brother Christmas' strategy was simple. His followers were poor and downtrodden and so he showed them somebody to tread upon. They, who had long felt inferior to everything, now felt superior to something. They cared not that they were not on top of the heap so long as there was a layer between them and the bottom. They became assertive, even violent, in their demands for priority over their so-called lesser human beings. There was an occasional riot and an increasing flow of bloodshed.

As the weeks went by, Clovis began to accept, then to preach, the poisonous doctrines of Brother Christmas. The Temple of the Golden Bird received nation-wide publicity, criticism and ridicule, but Clovis was immune to all this. He put all attacks down as the age-old attempt of the weak and the misguided to harass the strong and the enterprising. It did not even bother him that most outsiders gave no credence to the fact that he was a super-intelligent bird; that they considered him merely the second half of a vicious ventriloquist act.

"I'll bide my time," he said. "Some day they'll believe, and I'll have them in my power—from coast to coast."

This indicates how much territory was encompassed by Clovis in his dreams of grandeur. He was even getting ahead of Brother Christmas, who, in all modesty, wanted only California for his own. Of the two, Brother Christmas was the more intellectually honest. He knew he was a fake but Clovis was beginning to believe all his more favourable publicity.

On a certain Friday evening there was to be a 'monster super-rally' at the Temple of the Golden Bird. At this time a new edict was to be made public by Clovis. The edict concerned the banning of left-handed persons from membership in the temple and was to have been implemented by a campaign of vilification against the port-sided pariahs, but it never came off.

A few hours before the monster rally, Clovis, Thad, Grover and Brother Christmas were holding a business

139

conference. Honeybird was absent, having gone to her doctor to ascertain the reason for a slight nausea she had been experiencing of late. The conference had barely started when the door opened and in came August Von Lerner, travel-stained and weary.

"Ah, Clovis," he said, "it is you. That gold paint doesn't fool me."

"Of course it is I," declared Clovis. "What are you doing here, August? Why aren't you home in Oporto Freitas where you belong?"

"I have been reading about you," said August. "And what I read made me unhappy. Ah, to thnk that we, the Von Lerners, devoted generations of our lives to the breeding of a charlatan, a doer of evil!"

"I do not do evil," declared Clovis. "I do good. A million people love me."

"Nobody loves you," said August. "I was in the temple for your last sermon. You weren't inspiring love, you were inspiring hate. You were teaching people to hurt one another."

"To accomplish great good for the masses some people must be hurt," declared Clovis.

"Ah, Clovis, what a fool you are," sighed August. "I came here in the hopes of persuading you to change your ways but I see now that is impossible. There is no use in arguing with a fool, especially one drunk with power."

"Will one of you gentleman show Herr Von Lerner to the door?" asked Clovis coldly.

"I am stupid, as you well know," said August, "but in my years of contemplation, I have arrived at a few simple truths. You cannot elevate the human soul by appealing to all that is corrupt in human nature. You cannot benefit the masses by hurting even one of them, for if you hurt one you have hurt all. You cannot improve the lot of humankind through false hopes and promises, which, all too soon, give way to an eternity of disillusionment. Is there anything in your more brilliant philosophy that can refute that?''

''Please take him away,'' asked Clovis, more disturbed than he cared to admit.

''Not yet,'' said August. ''We, the Von Lerners, are responsible for you in all your evil, all your ugliness, all your rapacity. It is up to me, the last of the name, to destroy you. Ah, Clovis, how I loved you.''

With that he produced an ancient Luger revolver and aimed it at Clovis. Before he could fire, Brother Christmas knocked the weapon from his hand, then struck him several smashing blows in the face.

August stood there, bleeding and reeling.

''Ach,'' he said, ''what we Von Lerners have done to the world.''

He toppled to the floor and lay senseless.

Attendants were called in and they lifted him.

''I think he's gonna conk out for good,'' said one attendant as they carried him away.

''I,'' said Grover, ''feel the divine urge to drink.''

He produced a bottle and began drinking in mighty gulps.

*H*oneybird, in the meantime, was in the office of Dr Troyd. The doctor was examining her to determine the cause of the slight nausea. He was making a frightfully thorough job of it. There was something familiar in the liberties he was taking. Honeybird stared at his elbow and then gasped.

"I thought I recognised you," she said. "Didn't your name use to be Dr Haslett?"

"Why, yes," the doctor admitted, still buried in his work, "but I had to change it because of a slight professional mishap concerning a mix-up in prescriptions. Both patients died so I don't see what difference it made that they got the wrong medicine. Anyway the law is very narrow-minded so I adopted the name of Troyd. If you'll notice I also dyed my hair."

"So you have," said Honeybird and winced. "What are you doing now?" she asked.

"It's something I learned in medical school," said Dr Troyd. "I always do it."

"You mailed me a report," said Honeybird. "It changed my whole life."

"What report?" asked Dr Troyd, not looking up.

"About being barren and not attracted to the other sex," said Honeybird.

The doctor, the first time that afternoon, looked at her face.

"Now I remember," he said. "Boy, have I got something to tell you! You'll die laughing."

"What is it?" asked Honeybird.

"Well," said the doctor, "on the same day I examined you, there was a Miss Grobnisch in the office. Somehow or other I got your report mixed up with hers.

"Was her condition the same as mine?" asked Honeybird.

"Just the reverse," declared Dr Troyd. "The poor child, with your report, of course, went away from here convinced she was a nymphomaniac."

"She did?" asked Honeybird. "How awful."

"You'd be surprised at the time she had trying to live up to the report," chuckled the doctor. "She left a trail of neurotic young men from here to Nova Scotia."

"Then," said Honeybird, scarcely daring to believe, "I am *not* barren and unresponsive to the other sex?"

"Hell no," said the doctor.

"And I can get married?" asked Honeybird.

The doctor had finished his examination.

"You'd better," he told her.

*C*lovis was staring first at one and then at another of his human companions in the office of the Temple of the Golden Bird.

"Is it true? Is it anywhere near true—what August Von Lerner said?" he asked, hoping for reassurance.

Thad avoided his gaze. Grover had finished his bottle and was starting on the second.

"I'm drunk," he said. "I can't hear you."

"All great leaders are criticized," declared Brother Christmas. "Your August Von Lerner is merely a manifestation of—"

The door opened and a happy Honeybird came rushing in. She threw herself into Thad's arms.

"Oh Thad, dear Thad," she cried. "I don't have to simulate any more. We can be married."

She pulled his head down and she whispered into his ear. He smiled happily and then his face clouded.

"Oh, if you're thinking of that old money you can just forget all about it," said Honeybird. "I've just killed two birds with one stone."

"What do you mean?" asked Thad.

144

Honeybird dashed to the door and opened it.

"Come in," she called.

In came the beaming Miss Grobney, followed by the Prents and Beamish.

"Oh, the dear child," said Miss Grobney. "Did she tell you what she did, the clever little thing?"

"No," said Thad. "What?"

"She gave us the money," said Miss Grobney.

"*Gave* it to you?" asked Thad.

"Yes," said Lulu, "all that beautiful money."

"And now we do not have to-ah, shorten her days," said Sylvian happily.

"And at last I shall get my wages," said Beamish.

"And the horrid stuff won't stand between us any more," declared Honeybird to Thad.

"Well, I'll be damned," said Grover. "What a simple solution."

The four little grigs went out, babbling happily about how they were going to spend their beautiful money.

"It's against all human morality," Clovis told himself. "The evil should not be rewarded, they should be punished." He thought for a moment. "Yeah," he said to himself, "punished."

Thad lifted Honeybird off her feet and kissed her.

"I love you, Honeybird," he said fervently.

"Nobody but you could have thought of a thing like that."

He turned to the others.

"I'm leaving," he said. "I'm going far away. I'm going to have a son and I don't want him born within smelling distance of this stench."

"Where are you going?" asked Grover as they started out.

"Back to the jungle," declared Thad. "To make an honest living cheating the natives."

"I'll join you," said Grover. He stared at Clovis. "I can't see you, Clovis," he said. "I'm drunk and I don't believe in you any more. You never happened, you foul bastard."

He lurched happily out with Thad and Honeybird supporting him.

Brother Christmas turned to Clovis.

"Well," he said contentedly, "that leaves all the more swag for *us* to split up. Come on, Clovis, it's time for the revelation."

He lifted up the apathetic Clovis and carried him into the temple. He placed him on the golden throne and then made a long speech, warming the congregation up for the revelation.

"And now the great Clovis, bird of prophecy, speaks," he thundered.

Clovis stared in stony silence out over the sea of expectant faces.

"Fools," he said finally. "There is no money. No money. No money. Only *Work! Work! Work! Work! Work!*"

There was a babble of consternation.

"Work," repeated Clovis. "Work! Work! Work! Work!"

As Clovis kept bludgeoning them with that horrid word, the parishioners rose to their feet and started to shout in raw rage. Then they began to riot. Nothing Brother Christmas could do had any effect on them. They began to tear up seats, to break windows.

"Work!" shrilled Clovis. "Work! Work! Work! Work!"

Each repetition of the word served to increase their anger. They were berserk. Their rage was not that they had been robbed of their money; it was because they had been robbed of their dreams.

In a huge wave, they surged upon the platform and made for Clovis. Clovis flew away screaming, "Work! Work! Work! Work!"

Brother Christmas went down under a mass of flailing arms.

And then they began to kick him.

*A*s flames billowed up from the Temple of the Golden Bird, Clovis flew to the hospital where August Von Lerner had been taken. He entered the sickroom through an open window and, in a long conversation, made peace with August, who, it appeared, was not going to die after all.

"And now," said Clovis, after he had been forgiven, "I must leave you, my good August."

"Where to?" asked August.

"I go to seek my true destiny," said Clovis.

So firm was his tone that August realized that there was no use in arguing.

"Farewell, my Clovis," he murmured. "Farewell, sweet bird."

Clovis, by hitch-hiking rides on banana boats, finally made his way to the coast of Brazil. Then he flew mile after mile over the verdant jungle, seeking, seeking, seeking.

Finally he found what he sought. It was a flock of parrots, the same flock he had encountered before. He could tell by the presence of Red-Head.

The parrots squawked furiously as Clovis dropped down among them. There were cries of "Throw him out. Chase him away. We want none of him."

"Bear with me a moment," Clovis pleaded. "I have been away a long time. I have travelled many a weary mile. But I do not come here to relate my adventures. They are a closed book."

"Good, good," said the parrots.

Red-Head began pigeon-toeing toward Clovis.

"I come," said Clovis, "in all humbleness. I come as a supplicant. I ask you, my friends, to teach me how to be a parrot."

The others shouted for joy. Red-Head sidled up to Clovis.

And once again there was the heady odor of musk in his nostrils.